THE LAMBEG
AND THE BODHRÁN

THE LAMBEG AND THE BODHRÁN

DRUMS OF IRELAND

RINA SCHILLER

THE INSTITUTE OF IRISH STUDIES
QUEEN'S UNIVERSITY BELFAST
2001

First published in 2001
The Institute of Irish Studies, Queen's University Belfast
8 Fitzwilliam Street, Belfast, Northern Ireland, BT9 6AW

© Text, drawings and photographs, unless otherwise acknowledged,
Rina Schiller

This book has received support from the Cultural Diversity Programme
of the Community Relations Council, which aims to encourage acceptance and
understanding of cultural diversity. The views expressed do not necessarily reflect
those of the NI Community Relations Council.

British Library Cataloguing-in-Publication Data.
A catalogue record for this book is available from the British Library.

ISBN 0 85389 797 2

Page layout by Dunbar Design
Typeset in 11pt on 14pt Adobe Garamond
Printed by W & G Baird Ltd, Antrim

*To the
traditional musicians
of Ireland*

Contents

Acknowledgements

The Lambeg and the Bodhrán began as an academic project in 1994/95, when I was studying for my MA degree at Queen's University Belfast. During this initial phase of the project I discovered a rich variety of little-known details about the two drums, which led me into further research on the topic. Each phase of the project brought new discoveries, which lay more or less at my fingertips, but which had to be traced together from numerous different sources. At some stage I had become so deeply interested in the different musical traditions associated with the two drums, that no further purpose was required to make me continue my research.

I am particularly grateful to the Cultural Diversity Group of the Community Relations Council of Northern Ireland for their financial support during the final stages of the project, as this allowed me to carry it through to its printed form.

I am also very grateful to all those people who have shared their music and their information with me, and I feel glad and honoured to be able to give the accumulated knowledge back to the wider community in this processed and printed form. Numerous people have contributed to this project, without whose help this project would not have been possible, and I am grateful to them all. Although it is impossible to mention everyone by name, I would like to acknowledge at least some people who have been of particular help to this project.

Special thanks go to everyone who commented on drafts and made suggestions, in particular Desi Wilkinson, Margaret McNulty and Catherine McColgan; to Wendy Dunbar for her patience and design skills; to Críostóir MacCárthaigh, Bobby Magreechan, Gráinne McMacken, Cecil Kilpatrick and Frank Orr for help with photographs; to Kevin Danaher and the Department of Irish Folklore, University College Dublin, Jim Hamilton, Bobby Hanvey, Mrs Maureen Hewitt and Jill Jennings for permission to reproduce their photographs; to Comhaltas Ceoltóirí Éireann for their permission to take photographs at the Enniscorthy competitions; to Cormac for his permission to reproduce the cartoon; to all musicians and songwriters for permission to make transcriptions of their performances (although any possible inaccuracies are entirely my own fault); to Áine Nic Gearailt for help with translations from the Irish; to Suzel Reily for providing useful tips to locate specific ethnomusicological information; and to Tony Carver and Piers Hellawell for their helpful tips on transcriptions.

Further, I am grateful to the staff at Queen's University's Audio Visual Services (in particular Bill Mairs), to Queen's Computer Services, and to the staff of the Queen's Library (in particular the staff of Special Collections), for giving helpful advice and supporting my work in various ways.

Special thanks also to staff at the Ulster Folk and Transport Museum, in particular to Tony Buckley for valuable comments and help in sourcing materials, to Jonathan Bell for trying to arrange permission for taking a particular photograph, and to Fionnuala Scullion for permission to reproduce material from her article (1981) about the Lambeg drum.

I am also particularly grateful to Tommy Sands for helping to locate various musicians, to Tony Langlois for his encouragement, to Áine and Ralf Sotscheck for unearthing some source material under rather adverse conditions, to Helen Crickard from 'The Workshops' for providing numerous timber samples, to Peter Jahns for sending drawings which unfortunately got lost in the mail, to the Davey family for a lengthy journey to arrange accommodation, and indeed to everyone else who has contributed in some way to make this project possible.

RINA SCHILLER
NOVEMBER 2000

List of Illustrations

CHAPTER 2

CHAPTER 3

Sources of Illustrations

Unless otherwise stated the photographs, drawings and transcriptions are by the author. The author and publishers are grateful to the following people and institutions for giving permission to reproduce Fig. 1.12 Mrs Maureen Hewitt; Fig. 1.15 Jim Hamilton; Fig. 3.17 Bobby Hanvey; Fig. 4.3 Bobby Magreechan; Figs 4.7 and 4.8 the Head of Irish Folklore, the Folklore Department, University College Dublin; Fig. 5.1 Cormac; Fig. 5.5 Jill Jennings; and Fig. 4.4 Drumbeg LOL 638 and Cecil Kilpatrick.

PLATE 1:

'The Conqueror', made and decorated by Mark Hewitt around the beginning of the 20th century for the McCarthy family of Hillsborough. Later sold to the Lillie family of Hillsborough, and in the 1920s to LOL 722 Pond Park, the drum is now in the possession of instrument maker Frank Orr.

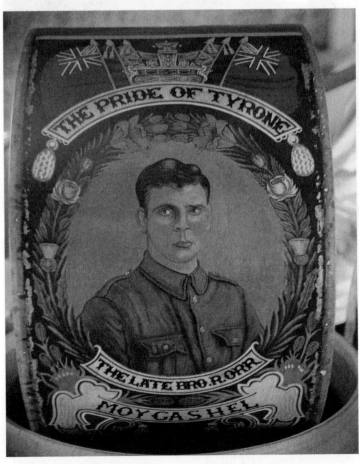

PLATE 2:

'Pride of Tyrone' memorial drum for Robert Orr (who died in the First World War), made and decorated by Mark Hewitt, Belfast (mid 20th century).

PLATE 3:
Tom Stewart from the Portadown area, playing
the 'Derrycorry Cock', made and decorated by
William Johnston (early 20th century).

PLATE 4:

AOH drum
'Owen Roe O'Neill'
from the Brantry area,
Co. Tyrone

PLATE 5:

AOH drum
'Brian Borou' from the
Belfast area

PLATE 6:
Eamon Maguire
drums with
individual hand-
crafted designs

PLATE 7:
Séamus O'Kane
drums with
differently cured
skins

PLATE 8:

Typical shading and
ornamentation of James
Davey's Bodhráns

PLATE 9:

Bass drum and side drums (Belfast 2000) played at
present-day Twelfth of July parades

Introduction

Drums are found in numerous cultures of the world. They are made in many different shapes and sizes, they are played in many different ways, and there is a multitude of different meanings attached to them, depending on their respective cultural contexts. The Lambeg and the Bodhrán are the only native drums played at present in Ireland. They both have a slightly ambiguous historical background, which intermingles with mythology and oral folk history, but they both have developed their present distinctive form, sound and associated playing styles in the geographical context of Ireland (north and south). Both drums have a variety of symbolic meanings ascribed to them. Symbolic meanings are socially constructed within society, and such meanings may change in accordance with changes within society. As far as the two drums are concerned, their symbolic meanings have indeed changed over time, but specific meanings also depend to a certain extent on their immediate social contexts. It may sound perhaps a bit tautological to state that a book of studies in musicology focuses rather on the musical aspects of the two drums than on the social construction of symbolic meanings. But on the other hand, there is a symbiotic relationship between instrument construction, playing styles, forms of decoration, and the social interpretation of their symbolic meanings within society. The latter aspect has been discussed in anthropological, sociological, and political texts, and for non-musicians it is perhaps not particularly relevant to inquire how musical meanings are constructed and transmitted within society. My interest lies with the musical aspects of the two drums and with the artistic process that takes place before a social interpretation of their results within society is possible. But since there is a reciprocal relationship between musical aspects and their social use and interpretation in society, I have integrated the latter to show their relevance for the development of instrument construction and playing styles of the two drums.

The approach I have chosen in this book is to start with a description of the features of the two instruments as they occur in present-day Irish society. The first chapter introduces a number of instrument makers of the Lambeg and the Bodhrán. The morphological features of the drums are described in detail in combination with the technological processes of their construction. Commonalities and differences between different instrument makers are pointed out, and there is also a section included on the construction of playing sticks for the instruments.

The next four chapters then introduce the various layers of meaning ascribed to the two drums within present-day society. It is not essential to read the chapters in the order in which they occur in the book. The sequence merely reflects my personal understanding of how different layers of meaning are ascribed to the drums. Using this social approach of looking at different layers of meaning, the second chapter introduces the different performance contexts where the Lambeg and the Bodhrán are used in present-day society. The third chapter looks in detail at different playing styles associated with the two instruments. It also discusses historical aspects which have led to the formation of these present-day playing styles.The fourth chapter investigates the history of the instruments and how particular meanings may have become attached to them. History can be seen from many different vantage points – e.g. ruling class/working class, rural/urban, male/female, written/oral – and since oral history and mythology are intimately interwoven with historical meanings of the drums, I found it impractical to subdivide these different aspects of history. Where historical data are taken from written records I have included the relevant references. As all versions of history are selective, the accounts given in this book are, of necessity, also selective. But since I had no intention to present any particular version of history – but rather as broad as possible a picture of different aspects relating to the two drums – it will be clear that this book is not to be understood as a 'historical' work. If it provides inspiration for future research on related topics it will well have served its purpose.

The fifth chapter then returns to present-day society and looks at how these various ascribed associations of the Lambeg and the Bodhrán are used by different artists within present-day society.

None of the chapters discuss *all* aspects in detail, which could have been investigated in relation to these topics. Rather, I have tried to give a broad overview of each topic by filling in as much fine detail as can be discussed in a book of this size.

It is the first book to be published which takes a comparative approach in looking at the two instruments, and I am indebted to various writers who have carried out previous research on either of the two instruments; in particular to Kevin Danaher, Mícheál Ó Súilleabháin, and Janet McCrickard for their research on the Bodhrán, and to Fionnuala Scullion for her detailed work on the Lambeg. I am also particularly grateful to all the instrument makers who have shared the many details of their craft with me, and also to the many musicians who have contributed their personal experiences of playing the drums within present-day society.

Coming from an ethnomusicological background, the comparative approach suggested itself to me, as both drums show some similarities in their construction, particularly in the materials which are used. The two instruments also have in common that they are associated with symbolic meanings within present-day society, and these have, in some contexts, come to stand as symbols for socio-cultural expressions. These symbolic meanings are not clear-cut, and they have also changed over time.

At various points in the text I have included direct speech descriptions, as I did not want to impose my own interpretation by summarising people's personal accounts in relation to what might seem most relevant at the present point in history.

One problem presented itself concerning musical transcriptions, as the musical genres discussed in this book are based on oral traditions. Choosing a particular form of transcriptions involves in itself a certain amount of interpretation. All world systems of transcriptions are based on symbolic representations of sound, and they will therefore all be selective by highlighting particular aspects of the music that is being transcribed. The standard western system of musical transcriptions has grown in close connection with the western art music tradition, and therefore it is most suited for written representations of music from this tradition. The system is therefore not particularly well suited for many fine details which occur in performances of traditional Irish music. Nevertheless standard western notation is often used by individual musicians as a mnemonic device to learn tunes, and also sometimes in the process of transmission. Taking all these aspects into consideration, I have decided to use an integrative approach. It consists of a combination of some standard notation with some genre-specific indications of performance details, to

which are added verbal descriptions of genre-specifically relevant stylistic details contained in these musical transcriptions.

In Chapter 3, I have transcribed some details of particular performances, as here my intention was to point out stylistic specifics in
these performances. The transcriptions are in no way to be understood as prescriptive. In Chapter 5, I have used transcriptions of only
basic melodies of songs – to give a broad idea of their musical shape
– as this chapter is not concerned with stylistic details, but with artistic uses of the images of the two drums within present-day society.
Most of the works discussed in this chapter are also commercially
available on CD or tape, and their details are given in the discography
at the end of the book.

Some technological factors concerning the drums – such as exact
pitch measurements – have deliberately been left out of this discussion, as neither drum is tuned to a particular pitch. Where pitch is
discussed in the text it relates to 'concepts of pitch', which are used
by musicians and audiences to describe particular sound qualities of
the drums. Within its own cultural contexts, the tuning of the drums
can therefore be said to be rather concerned with timbre and resonance than with a particular frequency.

All that remains to be said here is that I hope you will enjoy reading this book. It includes many different facets relating to the two
drums, and I hope everyone will find some interesting new aspects in
it. Of course, the music is best experienced in performance, and I
hope to meet you where the music is happening.

RINA SCHILLER
NOVEMBER 2000

The locations indicated on the map are the ones which are of particular relevance to the text. No conclusions should be drawn about their relative importance, or size, in relation to other locations in Ireland.

1
The craft of
instrument construction

 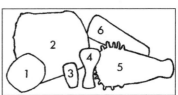

FIG. 1.1 KEY:

1 *Bodhrán* – Ireland
2 *Lambeg* – Ireland
3 *Moshupiane* (talking drum) – South Africa
4 *Darbuka* – Middle East
5 West African long drum
6 *Kendang* (Gamelan drum) – Bali. The *kendang* is played in pairs of a male drum *kendang lanang* and a female drum *kendang wadon*.

Drums are found in many cultures worldwide, and they are among the instruments which are commonly associated with symbolic meanings. Drums are made in different shapes and sizes and from different materials, but what they all have in common is that they are constructed from pieces of skin, which are stretched over a frame or body – the latter often of wood.

The Lambeg and the Bodhrán are two drums found in the island of Ireland. Traditionally they are both made from goatskin, stretched over a wooden frame or body. But although they both use the same materials, they are crafted in very different ways. The result is that one drum produces a high ringing sound, while the other produces a rather low sound, which is additionally damped in playing.

This chapter introduces instrument makers of both drums, and it explains how they use their craft to achieve these different sound qualities.

The Lambeg drum

The Lambeg drum is a large double-headed cylindrical drum, with provisions for tuning both heads to the same pitch. Its historical and morphological roots derive from the European side drum, of which Hornbostel and Sachs (1914) say that all of its forms have developed from the long cylindrical drum.

The present size of the Lambeg – as it is colloquially known – has been arrived at by much experimentation, and indeed such experiments are still ongoing. Its present dimensions are approximately 930mm in diameter across the head, and the width of the shell is about 610mm. Instrument maker Frank Orr relates that a drum of this size would be termed a 'three-foot one', but that their sizes do in fact vary within the range of around three-foot-one and three-foot-and-a-quarter. He describes instrument makers Hewitt's of Belfast as having made their drums measuring 3 foot $5/8$ inch, and that instrument makers Johnson's of Portglenone made their drums measuring 3 foot $7/8$ inch.

frame drum   cylindrical   kettle drum
              drum

CLASSIFICATION OF DRUMS

In western society the scientific classification of musical instruments is based on the Hornbostel-Sachs system, which identifies instruments by their method of sound production. This system divides instruments into five groups: idiophones, membranophones, chordophones, aerophones and electrophones.

Drums will generally fall into the category of membranophones, as their sound is produced by a vibrating membrane stretched over an opening. A sub-categorisation within this system would be to classify drums by their method of excitation (e.g. striking or friction), which is unsatisfactory, as some instruments may use a combination of these methods.

A more useful system is to distinguish drums by their different shapes (e.g. frame drums, cylindrical drums, kettle drums, goblet drums, cone drums, barrel drums, etc.), as the shape of a drum will influence its timbre and its sound amplification.

goblet drum   cone drum   barrel drum

The weight of a complete drum comes to around 42 pounds, or 19 kg, but occasionally slightly lighter drums are made on request. The shell of the drum is made of oak, and for its construction an instrument maker requires a 12 foot/360cm long plank of timber, which is 1 inch in depth and 12 inches wide. This plank is cut along the middle, and its two halves are placed aside each other to form a mirror image on the shell of the drum. Occasionally – when a suitable piece of timber is available – the shell is made out of one piece (as was the traditional way for constructing the drum), but the process described here of halving a plank is nowadays the common method used in its construction. On the inside of the shell these two halves are joined by a *centre hoop*, which is normally also made out of oak.

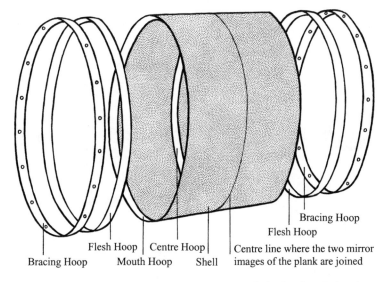

Bracing Hoop
Flesh Hoop
Flesh Hoop | Centre Hoop | Centre line where the two mirror
Bracing Hoop | Mouth Hoop | Shell | images of the plank are joined

FIG 1.2:
Lambeg shell and hoops

All the timbers used in the construction of the body of the drum must be steamed as part of the process of being turned into the desired shape. The steaming process is described on page 12 in more detail. As far as the shell is concerned, some instrument makers in the past have experimented with dry-turning the timber, hoping for a better sound from the drum. This method proved unsatisfactory, as the outside of the timber has to stretch for turning. The result was that it started to tear, while the inside of the shell tended to bend and warp. Consequently present-day instrument makers have returned to the method of steaming the timber for turning.

Different types of timber are used for the other hoops which are employed in the construction of the Lambeg drum. *Mouth hoops* are glued on along the edges inside the shell to give it stability and to provide a smooth edge for the skin to pass over. They are usually made from redwood or whitewood (Scandinavian or Canadian), or from Silver Spruce; i.e. from softwoods. Drummers would say about the *mouth hoops* that 'it is the softwood which puts the tone into the hardwood'. Mainly important for the choice of softwood timbers for *mouth hoop* construction would be their faultless condition (it must be free of knots), as the timber has to be turned round, and faulty timber cannot be turned, as it would break. Even if it were turnable it would not give the shell the desired stability.

The same type of timber is used for the *flesh hoops,* which are the hoops onto which the skin is lapped. These are then slipped over the edges of the drum. They are pressed down by the *bracing hoops/hall hoops,* which are brought into position and tightened by means of ropes. The *bracing hoops* are normally made of ash (hardwood). They need to be considerably stronger than the other hoops, as holes will

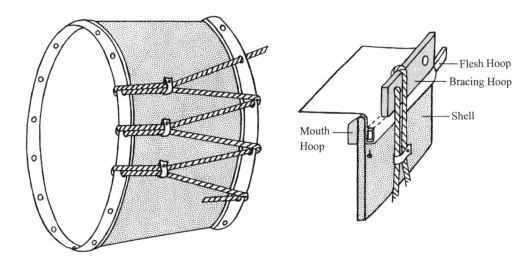

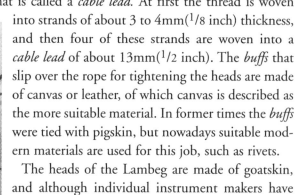

Flesh Hoop

Bracing Hoop

Shell

Mouth Hoop

Above left: FIG 1.3: Path of the ropes

Above right: FIG 1.4: Assemblage of the drum

be bored into them for the rope to pass through.

This rope was traditionally made of hemp, but nowadays linen or cotton is used, as legal barriers have arisen in relation to the importation of hemp. The material comes in spools of thread, and it is woven into what is called a *cable lead*. At first the thread is woven into strands of about 3 to 4mm(^{1}/8 inch) thickness, and then four of these strands are woven into a *cable lead* of about 13mm(^{1}/2 inch). The *buffs* that slip over the rope for tightening the heads are made of canvas or leather, of which canvas is described as the more suitable material. In former times the *buffs* were tied with pigskin, but nowadays suitable modern materials are used for this job, such as rivets.

The heads of the Lambeg are made of goatskin, and although individual instrument makers have experimented with other types of skins, they have always come back to goatskin – and in particular nanny-goat skin – as the best material for making the drum heads.

FIG 1.5: Instrument maker Richard Sterritt

Instrument maker Richard Sterritt from Markethill, Co. Armagh, has experimented with deerskin, but found it 'too high-pitched', and therefore as 'not producing the required resonance'. He also found it less suitable for tightening. According to Richard Sterritt's information skins of buck goats are also unsuitable, as they are usually too thick

FIG. 1.6:
Inside the shells the mouth hoops can be seen, and the centre hoop joining the two half-shells of a Lambeg drum. The two small pieces of timber on the left, inside the front shell, secure the attachment of the neck strap. The shells in the background also have their bracing hoops with them – loosely attached.

FIG. 1.7:
A selection of different types of hoops for the Lambeg drum. At the top of the picture a clamp has been attached to keep the timber firmly in position while drying out after having been joined.

FIG. 1.8:
Lambeg maker Richard
Sterritt attaches a clamp
for joining a newly made
half-shell.

and therefore too hard to work with. This point applies not only to the process of scraping the fat off the skin, but also in relation to the further working of the skin. Lambeg makers scrape the skin down to approximately the thickness of a sheet of paper, and even with an easily-workable skin the process of its preparation involves a considerable amount of work.

After the skin has been taken off the goat, it has to be cured. Lambeg makers do not use lime in this process – as Bodhrán makers do – since the Lambeg head requires a considerably higher tension, and lime curing would reduce the stability of the heads. Richard Sterritt points out that there are different ways of preparing the skin. As an example he describes one method in which all the hair is covered with horse manure and the skin is then rolled up inside a plastic bag, where it is left for two or three days. During this process the temperature inside the bag rises to about 60°C, and when the skin is taken out of the bag after a few days, the hair can easily be removed.

Afterwards the skin is washed, and then is ready for scraping. First the fat is taken off, and then the skin is dry-scraped with a wood-scraper, which takes off thin layers of skin. After this process the skin

FIG. 1.9:
Lambeg former.

For the process of joining, the half-shell is tightened around a former for drying out – to give it an even shape.

is watered again, and then lapped onto the *flesh hoops*. The final stage of the preparation of the skin was described by Richard Sterritt in these words : 'And then you put the stuff on to put the music in with. I can't tell you what that is'. This process is known as the 'doping' of the skin. A special mixture is applied to the skins, the ingredients of which are a closely guarded secret of all instrument makers. Various people mentioned to me that one of the ingredients is of high alcoholic content, but the other ingredients vary considerably between different instrument makers. It is also said that most drummers additionally apply their own mixture to the drum heads, especially before drumming competitions (cf. Scullion 1982:19).

Richard Sterritt works on Lambeg drums with his brother Roly and his nephew Darren Sterritt. Like most instrument makers, the Sterritts have a background in joinery and woodwork, and they give regular workshops on the playing of the instrument in Markethill, across the country, and further afield. Apart from repairing and restoring old drums, the Sterritts make their own instruments, which they number. As far as skins are concerned, the Sterritts favour a bell-like sound in their drums.

As the skins are the most essential component in producing varieties in the timbre of drums, great care is given to their preparation. Over a ton of pressure works on the middle of the heads when the drum is ready for playing and therefore the skin has to be prepared and attached very carefully. On the other hand, the very thinness of the heads makes the Lambeg extremely susceptible to changes in temperature and moisture content in the air. In fact Richard Sterritt

FIG. 1.10:
Instrument maker Frank Orr

FIG. 1.11:
Lambeg maker Frank Orr prepares a
new skin. The skin is scraped down
with a woodscraper, to give it its
required thinness.

refers to the Lambeg as a 'big barometer', because from the sound of the heads and the process involved in their tuning he can sense the air pressure and moisture in the air and so predict the weather.

When a new skin is put on a drum, care will be taken to ensure that the spine mark lies at right angles to the playing position, as this will give the drum head its highest stability in playing. The tuning of a drum is a rather complicated procedure, which is described in Chapter 3.

Lambeg maker Frank Orr comes from a long line of at least three generations of drum makers. Frank now lives in the Tandragee area, but his family roots are in Lambeg, Co. Down. Frank says that he learnt the family tradition of instrument construction by 'giving the older people a hand with their work' when he was a youngster. This tradition reaches well back into the nineteenth century, and he is also familiar with the older procedures of working with drums. According to Frank's description the 'old masters' did not talk much about their craft, and they used mostly natural ingredients in working the skins. Nowadays, he describes instrument makers as getting their ingredients from the chemist's, but Frank thinks that 'the use of some chemicals' is a good idea, providing you 'don't dabble away from nature too far'.

A central ingredient in the first part of the curing process is ammonia which is nowadays obtained from a chemist's shop. If other ingredients are used – those which the Lambeg makers term 'chemicals' to differentiate them from natural ingredients – the hair will come off the skin in one day. The skin is then washed thoroughly, stretched unto a board, and the back scraped down with a woodscraper. Afterwards the skin is soaked again in water, and then stretched onto a *flesh hoop*. At this time the skin will be 'doped', and the particular mixture of ingredients used in this process will essentially influence the sound qualities of the skins. This process is described as 'putting the music in'.

Frank describes the quality of the water as also quite important.

> You mightn't think it, but you need the really good hard spring
> water. That's where you get the most change in the skin. Water com-
> ing out of a well where there's limestone – you can't beat it. That
> would give you what you would call a high-pitch sound in a drum.

During the last stage of the process the skins
should not stay too long in the water, because
otherwise they will thicken. Frank recounts that
in the old days people would then have kept the
skins for about a year – for what they would call
the 'seasoning process' – before they would have
tried them on a drum.

Nowadays the 'seasoning process' is usually
shorter, as instrument makers use slightly different ingredients in the curing process.
Another significant change in modern times is
that it is not just instrument makers who produce drumheads; there are also a few people
around who experiment just with skins, as
Frank describes:

> For a long time there was only Johnson's and
> Hewitt's, really, but now there's a lot of people at
> it. There's a lot of folk making their own skins and making skins for
> other people. And make them in different ways, you know?
> Different tans, and using different sorts of chemicals and things like
> that.

FIG. 1.12:
Instrument maker
William Hewitt
(1922–1991) in the
1960s

So the process of experimentation is very much alive today, and skins
that give a really outstanding sound are highly desired for taking a
drum to competitions, as the skins are an essential element in the
production of a 'good sound quality' in an instrument.

Jimmy Cousley from Aldergrove, Co. Antrim, is best known within drumming circles for making the sticks used nowadays for playing
the Lambeg. Jimmy told me that originally he had been inspired by
Eamon Maguire (the Bodhrán-maker discussed later in this chapter)
to start his craft. By now the excellent quality of his sticks is known
far and wide, and they are much sought after. Jimmy said that he did
not share the view of the older generation of instrument makers, who
kept their craft a secret, since because of this, many of the old crafts

died out. He told me in detail how he makes his sticks, so that people may learn to make their own.

Stick making is a lengthy procedure, requiring considerable patience and a variety of materials. The essential material is malacca

cane, a high quality cane of a brownish colour. White cane can also be used, if it provides the right size and length of material without knots, though malacca cane is generally of a better quality. The cane is imported from overseas, and when it arrives it is fairly dry. The cane is then cut into pieces of 45 to 55cm (18 to 22 inches) – the desired length for playing sticks – and steeped for two or three months in a jar of oil (e.g. linseed oil). This gives the canes their flexibility.

To make these canes into sticks, at first the end is steeped into a sealer (Jimmy uses a sealer which was used for the canvas of old aircraft), and a ring of fibre board is placed at the end for building up the layers of padding. Then shammy leather is cut into thin strips, and six or seven layers of these strips are glued around the end of the cane with

FIG. 1.13:

Lambeg drum and stick maker Jimmy Cousley winds flax around the grip of a new stick, which is in the process of being made.

Evo-stick (528). The last layer consists of flax, to give the grip of the stick an even shape. At this point the sticks are left overnight to dry thoroughly. The next day a layer of rubber is added over the padding. For this layer Jimmy uses the material which is employed for tennis racket handles. Then both ends of the grip have to be trimmed. The outside end is covered with a patch of felt-like material (a piece of calender blanket) that is stitched on around the edge and coloured (usually black) to match the rubber. The inner end – where the cane emerges from the grip – is secured by heavy thread, which is wound around the end of the cane and the padding, and it is secured by a self-tightening knot. This thread is then also coloured in a matching shade and sealed with the aircraft sealer.

The last part of the process is the trimming of the top of the stick. It is first rounded off with a file, then smoothed with fine sandpaper, and then dipped into oil to bring back its colour. Having been sealed, finally the stick is finished off with a coat of French polish. Of course, the sticks are made in pairs. So for each pair the canes and grips have to be matched in length, width, and weight. The standard stick length for adult drummers lies at around 22 inches, but some people prefer slightly shorter sticks (especially children), and there are also varying tastes concerning the weight of the sticks.

Like most instrument makers, Jimmy has a woodworking background, and he has also made a few drums. He showed me his steamer construction, where he steams the timber to turn it into the desired shape.

FIG. 1.14:
Self-tightening knot

FIG. 1.15:

Lambeg drum and stick maker Jimmy Cousley attaches a piece of timber coming out of the steamer to a wheel, for turning it into the desired shape.

Steamers cannot be bought 'over the counter'; the instrument maker has to assemble them from various odds and ends. In the photograph on page 11, Jimmy is holding a piece of timber coming out of the steamer, which is being clamped onto the wheel in front, for turning. At the back of the steamer an oven is attached, where water can be heated to produce the steam. In Lambeg making the steaming of timber is essential, as solid timber is used, and the steaming process makes the timber soft and pliable. After the timber has been prepared in this way, a former is required to turn the timber into the desired shape. Timber treated in this way keeps its shape afterwards and gives the instrument good stability.

When Lambeg makers acquire good pieces of skin which are too small for Lambeg heads, they will usually sell them to Bodhrán makers, as the Bodhrán has a considerably smaller head. Most instrument makers concentrate on the construction of either drum only, but occasionally people make both types of drums. An example is James (Jimmy) Hamilton (deceased) from Carrickfergus, Co. Antrim, who worked with drums for about 25 years, and who made Bodhráns from the smaller-size materials that were left over in the process of Lambeg making. James is remembered as an easy-going and humorous person by many instrument makers, musicians and drumming aficionados. An anecdote is told about him being interviewed by Walter Love for a local radio programme. When suddenly the lights in the room started flashing, James explained to Walter that this just meant that 'the wife was telling them the tea was ready'.

FIG. 1.16: Instrument maker Jim Hamilton (1929–1995) and brother William (front right) adjusting a drum with family friend Aubrey O'Neil (left).

The Bodhrán

The Bodhrán is a comparatively small, hand-held frame drum with a single head. Nowadays the diameter across its head usually measures between 14 and 20 inches, and its frame depth varies between 3 and 6 inches. The smaller the head of the instrument, the harder the sound will be, as resonance decreases with head size. The head size is therefore of crucial importance for the sound of the instrument, since in frame drums it is essentially the skin that produces the sound, as their body does not enclose vibrating air and so plays a small part in the amplification of the sound.

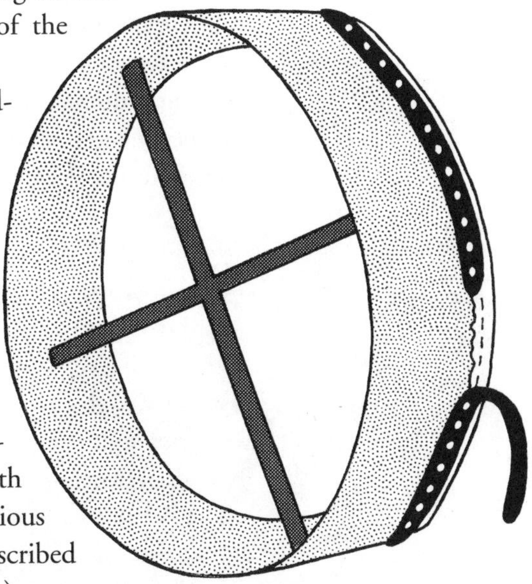

The size of the drum is in no way standard-ised, and its head is not tuned to any particu-lar pitch. Size and skin tension are rather determined in relation to the most effective sound concerning timbre, loudness, and res-onance. As in the case of the Lambeg drum, ideas of a 'good sound' are related to tradi-tional ideas of its timbre, but the spectrum of what is regarded as a 'good sound' is con-siderably wider, allowing for variety in indi-vidual taste. Some Bodhráns are provided with devices for tightening the skin. There are various tuning systems in existence; these will be described later in more detail. (See box feature page 24.)

FIG. 1.17:
The Bodhrán

The frame of the drum is made of wood. The older generation of Bodhrán makers often used the frames of household riddles, to which they attached a goatskin. Another method was to use old bar-rels, to which the skin was tacked for drying and stretching. When the skin was ready the top slice of the barrel was cut off, thereby pro-viding a ready-made frame. Jim Humphries (1976:19) describes Frank McNamara of Ennistymon, Co. Clare, as having used this method.

Often, the older generation of instrument makers inserted jingles into the rim. These were made from pennies, or the like, which were hammered flat, but not too flat for jingling, as Bodhrán maker James Davey describes. Nowadays various different types of timber are used for making Bodhrán frames: oak, ash, beech, birch (hardwoods); solid woods or plywoods. When using solid woods the process of turning involves steaming, but often thin layers of plywood are used, which can be turned round without steaming. For achieving a good amount of stability without making the instrument too heavy for handling in playing, the thickness of the frame is usually made at around 9mm ($3/8$ inch).

The overlapping edges of the timber are planed and sanded down to fit smoothly over each other. The timber is then turned around a former, glued together, and kept in position by a clamp while drying out. A strap is a useful device for tightening around a frame to press it onto a former, as it exerts an even pressure around the whole frame. When the frame is dried out its edges are smoothed down, and a cross-piece of oak (or other hardwood) is inserted, which gives the frame additional stability. The cross-piece is also important for the playing of the Bodhrán, as it helps to position the player's hand in relation to the skin.

The cross-piece may consist of a single bar, of a T-shaped construction, or of an actual cross-shaped piece. Older drums often had only two crossing pieces of wire attached inside the rim, but nowadays cross-pieces are generally made of wood; although some Bodhráns have no cross-piece at all. Some Bodhrán makers produce instruments of an individual style, while others experiment with a variety of styles. The specific differences are discussed in relation to individual instrument makers.

The skin itself is most often goatskin (regarded as traditional), but deerskin is also quite popular, and greyhound or donkey have also been described as giving good results (Shaw-Smith 1984:110). Eric Cunningham (1999:16) describes goatskin as the most popular choice of skin, which is favoured for its sound qualities, its durability and its skin thickness. According to his research, some Bodhrán makers also use deer, greyhound, sheep, calf, stillborn ass, or horse skin in the manufacturing process.

Greyhound skin seems indeed to give very good results, as Mícheál Ó Súilleabháin (1974a:4–7) mentions two Bodhrán makers (Sonny Canafin from the Listowel region, Co. Kerry, and Paddy Lawlor from Ballingarry, Co. Tipperary) who described greyhound skin as the best possible choice. And James Davey – the Bodhrán maker discussed later in detail – told me that, although he always used goatskin for his instruments, he had been baffled by the excellent sound qualities when he heard a greyhound skin Bodhrán being played.

Bodhrán maker Charlie Byrne from Thurles, Co. Tipperary, told me in the 1970s that he mostly used goatskins on his instruments, but that he had also made some deerskin Bodhráns. Belfast Bodhrán maker Eamon Maguire describes deerskin as giving a harder tone than goatskin, but that this aspect could not be regarded as attributing to 'better' or 'less good' sound qualities of an instrument, as the choice of preferred tone will depend on the individual player's taste.

There is a standard method (lime) and various alternative methods in existence to cure the skins. While one Bodhrán maker who learnt his craft from Charlie Byrne told me that he had been inspired by him to use different curing methods, another Bodhrán maker who also learnt his craft from Charlie Byrne believes that the different curing methods are 'part of the myth which Charlie Byrne likes to create around himself'. As Charlie Byrne is a man of many facets, it is maybe just as well that he was not available for comments on this topic, as he may well choose to tell different things to different people, and mine might yet have been another version.

The normal curing process takes about ten days, and when the skin is cured the fat and hair can be removed with a scraper. While the skin is still moist and pliable it is stretched onto the frame, temporarily tacked on, and left to dry for about four days, or longer. (James Davey would have left the skins to sit for up to six months.) After this period it is then either tightened up or slackened off to give it the suitable tension, and nailed onto the frame with upholstery nails. Some instrument makers additionally glue the skin to the frame, but this method has the disadvantage that the skin cannot be adjusted at any point in the future.

Most Bodhrán makers also produce playing sticks for the instrument, the most common of which is a double-ended wooden stick of about 20 to 25cm (9 inches) in length. Individual musicians prefer different shapes and sizes of sticks, but often they are made from hardwoods, and they are turned on a lathe. The most important aspect is that they are well balanced for playing, although James Davey told me that he used to carve the sticks by hand (from broom handles), and that he preferred to use softwood. He said that Kevin Conneff and some other musicians had described softwood sticks as giving 'a better sound'. In playing, James Davey attaches the stick with an elastic band to his middle finger. This is a not so widespread method of playing the Bodhrán, and softwood may indeed be more suitable for this playing style (and not just a matter of personal taste). The different playing styles are discussed in Chapter 3.

Eamon Maguire is a Belfast instrument maker who – like most Bodhrán makers – started his craft in the 1960s.

In a 1995 radio broadcast[1] Eamon describes how he was first attracted to the playing of the drum in Co. Clare at around 1960:

---

[1] Part 3 (The Bodhrán) of the six-part series 'Instruments of Ireland', produced by Ian Kirk-Smith, and presented by Tony McAuley. It was first broadcast on BBC Radio Ulster in 1995.

The first time I really saw a drum getting played was in Doolin… And the old boy who was playing it, he was an oldish sort of man, and he was playing one with pennies… And he played with his hand. And he used a technique of playing that, when he was playing, he used to rub his thumb up the skin, and it made the pennies tremble.[2]

FIG. 1.18:
Instrument maker
Eamon Maguire

The instrument which Eamon describes here is indeed constructed in the same way as many Bodhráns made in the 1920s and 1930s, for instance by instrument maker James Davey. The Doolin Bodhrán had no cross-bar; it had 'just a couple of pieces of wire across the back', and in playing it was held by the rim.

I asked Eamon how he had started off making Bodhráns. As an early influence he mentions Charlie Byrne, whom he first met at the Newport Fleadh, Co. Tipperary, in 1968.

I started making drums about 1967. At first I made a drum for myself. I went to a fleadh in Enniscorthy [Co. Wexford, 1967], and I played a drum there. And when I came home I made one for myself. Then a fellow, Mick Burn, asked me to make one for him, and I made one for him. And then it sort of snowballed from there. I first met Charlie Byrne the following year [1968] at the Newport Fleadh in Tipperary. He was the only influence on me at the time, and I met him afterwards every year. Then at around 1968/69 I decided that I would need a workshop, and I got one in York Lane, off Upper Donegall Street. I was there for twelve years, and a great wee place it was. Then I moved up to the Brookfield Mill, as the other place was being knocked down because of redevelopment.

2 Incidentally, this is a playing technique employed by the Brazilian (Folia de Reis) Christmas rhymers/mummers, who go from house to house with their performances to collect money, to be used for a following community festival. The same playing technique is not employed in any other Brazilian genre of music, although Brazilian genres widely make use of the tambourine.
  For a detailed discussion of the Brazilian Folia de Reis tradition please see S. Reily (1995, and forthcoming).
  The congruence of playing styles may well be coincidental, but it is also possible that it travelled – and was transmitted within – different rhymers/mummers traditions. The Folia de Reis tradition is said to have originated from Portugal, and Eamon Maguire's guess about Middle Eastern connections of this playing style may well have its historical roots in a connection between these different rhymers/mummers traditions.

At the time of writing Eamon is moving into new premises in 497 Antrim Road, in the Fortwilliam area of Belfast. The Brookfield Mill is a huge complex, which houses a number of community crafts and other workshops. The new premises are situated above a row of small shops, and they will certainly provide easier access for visitors looking for the Bodhrán-maker's workshop.

Eamon makes different sizes of Bodhráns, but nowadays the most popular instruments are those of the 18-inch diameter size. Each instrument is hand-crafted as described in the following paragraphs, and the decorated drums carry individual handmade designs. Usually Eamon leaves a tiny bit of fur on the skin for decoration.

For the construction of the frame two layers of plywood are smoothed down, glued together, and placed around a former. Then the rim is left to dry out,

FIG. 1.19:
Bodhrán maker Eamon Maguire planes down the edges of a piece of timber, to make a smooth joint for a Bodhrán frame.

FIG. 1.20:
For the process of joining, the timber is tightened around a former for drying out – to give it an even shape.

before the next step can be carried out. And then, of course, a good skin will be required, which has to be processed beforehand. When I asked Eamon how to start making a Bodhrán, his description evoked images of bravery, hunting skills, and a celebrational meal:

'You go and shoot the goat, skin it – and eat the goat'.

Many Bodhrán makers point out that wild goats provide the best skins, but that they are extremely difficult to catch. Either way you will have to kill the goat in such a way that the part of the skin which is to be made into drums is not damaged. You may, of course, be extremely lucky – as Charlie Byrne put it, when he spoke to me in the 1970s – to come across a goat that has been knocked down on the road. Alternatively, some Bodhrán makers import their skins from countries where a lot of goats meat is consumed. Not every animal killed in our own culture – nor indeed in other cultures – is given the honour of a celebrational meal in combination with being made into a musical instrument.

For curing the skins Eamon Maguire describes the standard procedure of leaving the skin in a lime solution for about ten days, so that afterwards the hair can be removed. But sometimes Eamon will add a bit of sour milk which, he says, 'does a bit of curing as well'.

After removing the fat and hair the skin is not scraped further down; it is used with whatever thickness it has. The thickness will, of course, vary depending on the animal, so that different tastes of musicians are catered for. Eamon considers skins of a one-year-old buck goat or a two-year-old nanny goat as exceptionally good.

When the rim around the former has dried out it is treated with wood dye, French polish, and finally with varnish. Then it has to be left to dry again, before the skin can be tacked on for the stretching process.

After the skin has been stretched, its tension is adjusted and it is permanently fixed to the frame. Like most modern-day Bodhrán makers, Eamon uses a decorative band and brass upholstery nails for this purpose. During excessively busy periods Eamon has one or two young helpers working with him. But he always provides the finishing touch himself, and the final skin decoration is entirely done by himself. For specific skin decorations see colour plate 6 on page xviii.

Apart from the standard model, Eamon also produces tunable Bodhráns on demand. The system which Eamon uses requires a lot of work, but it allows a nice and easy tuning of the instrument without any danger of overstretching the skin. Eamon's tunable Bodhráns

Opposite top
FIG. 1.21:
Two Bodhrán frames made from the same type of timber. The front frame has been treated with wood stain, French polish, and varnish. The back frame is still in its natural state.

Opposite bottom
FIG. 1.22:
Bodhrán maker Eamon Maguire lays down the ground pattern for the skin decoration of a new instrument.

FIG. 1.23:

If requested, Eamon Maguire provides his instruments with an inner hoop and sliding wedges, which serve to adjust the skin tension to changing air conditions.

contain an inner hoop, which is pressed onto the skin by means of sliding wedges – thereby tightening the skin and consequently raising its pitch. The pegs for the sliding wedges are made of hardwood, usually oak.

Hardwoods are also used for making the cross-piece; as well as for stick making, for which Eamon uses a lathe.

Eamon travels widely to give workshops on the Bodhrán. These include information on playing techniques, instrument construction, and on the historical and cultural background of the drum. He also travels to fleadhanna (sometimes anglicised as fleadhs) to sell his instruments – as indeed many instrument makers do – and he teaches his customers playing techniques for the Bodhrán.

Belfast musician and Bodhrán teacher Gavin O'Connor recounts a story about a fleadh in Buncrana, Co. Donegal, at which Eamon provided a free Bodhrán lesson to two potential customers, who then left without buying an instrument. Later on that evening Eamon and Gavin went to the local pub for a music session. The pub was packed

FIG. 1.24:
A selection of sticks of different shapes and sizes for playing the Bodhrán. Eamon Maguire turns his sticks on a lathe.

with excellent musicians when they arrived. Among them were Eamon's two 'customers', banging 'with big wooden lumps on plastic water containers'. When they spotted Eamon they started praising him in loud voices as their percussion teacher. It is said that Eamon did not particularly appreciate their praise.

Séamus O'Kane from Lower Drum near Dungiven, Co. Londonderry, made his first Bodhrán in the late 1960s. Like Eamon, he refers to Charlie Byrne as an early influence, but also to James Davey, both of whom he describes as the best-known Bodhrán makers at this time. Séamus tells a story about how he first met Charlie Byrne at a fleadh in Ennis, Co. Clare, in 1977.

> I played at the fleadh in Ennis, and this man was always sitting behind me at the sessions I was playing. And in the pub at the end then he said he was from Thurles. And I said, 'Oh, I'm down here to try and find a man from Thurles. I'm going to travel over to Thurles tomorrow.' He says, 'What does he do?' And I says, 'He's a Bodhrán maker. And I'm not entirely sure what his name is. I was only told it once.' And he says, 'Do you remember his first name or his second name?' And I says, 'His first name is Charlie.' And then he says, 'It wasn't Byrne by any chance?' And I says, 'Aye.' And he says, 'You're talking to him.'

Séamus describes how he was particularly influenced by Charlie Byrne's different methods of curing skins. He likes to experiment with curing processes, and he uses at least three different methods. But Séamus has also been influenced by Lambeg makers, and his skins are indeed so thin that his instruments constitute something like a cross-over between Lambegs and Bodhráns. His instruments are much sought after by musicians who perform in front of microphones rather than in sessions, as the thin skins are regarded as more responsive for fine ornamentation and better suited for sound amplification.

Séamus seldom uses lime to cure skins. One material he does use for curing is oak bark, which is left for one or two days in water, and in which the skins are then steeped for eight to ten days. The other material he uses for curing skins is tallow, which makes the skin look white and fatty, and indeed emits drops of fat. But Séamus also has

FIG. 1.25: Instrument maker Séamus O'Kane

a drum on which he used tallow first, then lime, and then tallow again.

Séamus describes how he and Gino Lupari developed a high-pitched sound in Bodhráns by using chemically cured Lambeg skins (Hobson skins).

FIG. 1.26:
A modern Séamus O'Kane Bodhrán (left) and a 1970s Charlie Byrne Bodhrán (right). Although the proportions of the instruments are different, their construction and decoration are essentially the same.

FIG. 1.27:
Cured and dried skins can be stored until they are required for making a Bodhrán. After checking the size of the skin and the frame in relation to each other, the skin is watered for a short period, before it is stretched onto the frame.

FIG. 1.28:
Séamus O'Kane shows a Bodhrán provided with his turnable tuning pegs. Beside these sits an element from a cam tuning system, which works in a manner similar to Eamon Maguire's sliding wedges.

The tuning of his instruments is aided by a rim system with tuning pegs. Séamus considers eight tuning pegs as optimal for a good tuning of the instrument. In the photograph Séamus shows an older tuning system – called a cam – beside the pegs of his own tuning system. But learning how different curing methods affect the sound of the drums did not come easy to him. Séamus tells a story from his early days of Bodhrán making, around 1969, during his first year of working as a teacher in a local school. Séamus had heard about a great method of curing skins to achieve particularly good sound qualities:

I was reading an article in an Irish music magazine. And it said that they were burying the skin in the bog to give it particular qualities. But it wasn't right. They were burying it in the bog to keep away the worms, cause there's no worms in the bog. So that no worms will attack the skin. That will allow them to keep it buried for about ten days, and then it decomposes to a certain amount, and the follicle allows the hairs to pull out. And I did it that way once. And there's an awful awful smell. And I just couldn't get rid of the smell for a good few days. But once I got the skin I was so eager to get it made [the Bodhrán], that I took it to work with me. And I just had to have it done there and then. But the headmaster had a very sensitive sense of smell. He was away at the far end of the building, talking to a teacher, and he said, 'What's that terrible smell?' I had the Bodhrán hung in the window of the classroom to dry, you see? And the wind was carrying the smell into the corridor, and he [the headmaster] followed his nose right round the school to come to my room. And he saw the drum, and he says, 'Is that what it is? You better get it out of here, and as quickly as possible!'

FIG. 1.29: Different tuning systems of the Bodhrán

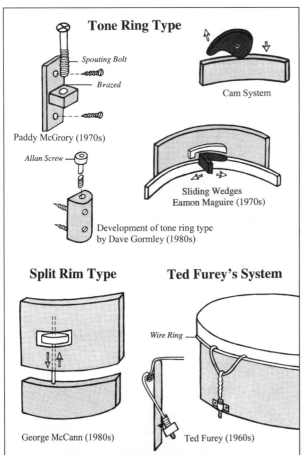

Tone Ring Type

Spouting Bolt

Brazed

Cam System

Paddy McGrory (1970s)

Allan Screw

Sliding Wedges
Eamon Maguire (1970s)

Development of tone ring type by Dave Gormley (1980s)

Split Rim Type

Ted Furey's System

Wire Ring

George McCann (1980s)

Ted Furey (1960s)

Séamus O'Kane's Bodhrán heads are slightly smaller (about $15\,1/2$ inches) in diameter than the average heads, but his frames are about 6 inches wide, a good bit wider than in most Bodhráns nowadays. This puts his drums close to becoming cylindrical drums. Technically speaking, a drum is considered to be a frame drum when its rim is narrower than half the diameter of its head. When the rim grows wider the instrument becomes a cylindrical drum; and with this its body becomes more influential in its sound amplification. Séamus always decorates his frames with a dark wood-dye, and he uses no decoration on his skins. If he attaches a cross-bar, it is a single cross-piece.

Another of his unique features is the addition of a few layers of tape around the outer edges of the drum head. According to Séamus this idea comes from Peadar Mercier, and it is said to make the instrument 'more controlable'. Séamus also describes Peadar Mercier as an early influence in the development of his tuning system. Peadar Mercier is reported to have invented a system for tuning his own instrument in the late 1960s. The traditional instruments had been quite susceptible to cold and damp weather conditions; a distinct disadvantage for musicians playing Bodhráns in stage performances. But, according to Séamus, it was Ted Furey who constructed the first tunable Bodhrán, and his was a system for tuning the instrument from the outside.

Séamus O'Kane can be heard playing the Bodhrán on recordings with Tomás Ó Canainn, Harry Bradley, John Wynne, and on a live recording from the Crosskeys Inn, Co. Antrim.

Paraic McNeela is a Dublin Bodhrán maker, who also relates that he was taught by Charlie Byrne in his early years of instrument construction. Like other Bodhrán makers, he met Charlie at different fleadhanna. The first of these meetings he describes as having taken place in 1979 or 1980 at the Willie Clancy Week in Miltown Malbay, Co. Clare. Paraic describes how he learned a lot over time through talking to Charlie Byrne, and says that he used to get skins from him. Until a few years ago Paraic was still working from home. But in recent years his business has expanded to such an extent that he has acquired a workshop unit in a Dublin industrial estate at Baldoyle.

Paraic constructs Bodhráns of very varied appearances, with and without skin decoration, and he told me that he likes to experiment with different tones and timbres of the instrument. A speciality of his invention is a tunable double-skin Bodhrán, in which both skins are lying against each other with their rough sides inwards. On his tunable models Paraic uses five pegs with knobs for turning them.

FIG. 1.30:
Instrument maker
Paraic McNeela

When I asked Paraic to tell me some details about his craft he started by talking about goats:

Firstly, goats are not killed for the skin. The skin is a by-product. In Ireland goats are generally used to run with cattle in fields, and it's the goat that will eat the bad grass, and the cattle eat the good grass. When the farmer doesn't need the goats anymore, or maybe he wants to cull out of the herd, he would send them off to a goat herder, who would butcher the goats for dog meat. And the goat meat is used to rear greyhounds. And the skin is a by-product; it's either thrown out, or it's sold to a Bodhrán maker.

Paraic then gives a detailed account of curing skins in a barrel of lime, which is more or less the same procedure as that described by Eamon Maguire. To this he adds that, after the lime has been washed out of the skins, he would put them into a pickle barrel of brine (water and salt) to finish off the curing and to get rid of any remaining smells in the skins. Then the skin will have to be dried, either in the open air – in sunny weather it may be bleached white – or in an outhouse or a farmshed. Paraic continues:

When the skin is dried it becomes very hard, and also all the oils have been cured out of the skin. So it's a good idea at that stage to put some oils back into it. Now, many oils can be used: linseed oil, or baby oil, or dubbin, raw linseed oil. Bees wax and vaseline is excellent. Vaseline on its own is excellent. Even cooking oil is good,

FIG. 1.31:

After a short period of watering the skin is tacked onto a Bodhrán frame for stretching. When the skin has dried out, its tension will be adjusted for its desired sound properties, before it is permanently nailed to the rim.

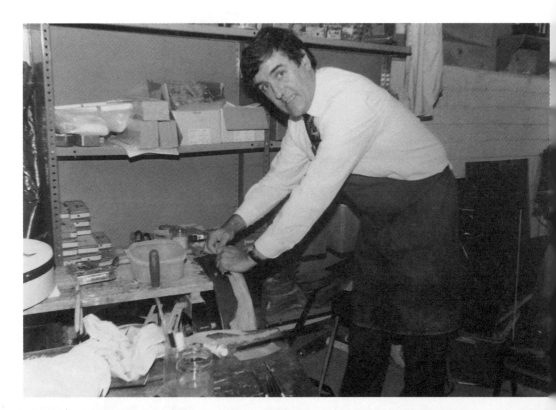

or a body cream, or hand cream, or any of those. You would treat it the way you would treat your own skin; which is probably the best way to do it. And then finally you put some nice-smelling oil on it. If you're in a session and it's still too hard you would just wet the back of the skin with water. And the more the skin is played the softer and more subtle it becomes.

I asked Paraic what type of skins he would consider to make particularly good Bodhráns. This is how he described it:

> Some people like to use a goatskin which gives a real hard tone – which would be a puck goat, an old man goat. Other people like to use the female goat, because the skin is more subtle, and you can get more subtle soft sounds out of it. So it depends on the person. Everybody is looking for something different. Even, not only in goat skins, but in beaters. You'd have Bodhrán players who would have a selection of beaters, and it's just to what suits them. It becomes very personal; it's like a painting. People judge a Bodhrán much the same way as a painting. It becomes very personal to the person who's playing it.

Paraic also makes playing sticks of different sizes, but in addition he sells some two-coloured sticks made by Dave Harper, another Dubliner. The two-coloured sticks are made by laminating different

FIG. 1.32:

Paraic McNeela makes Bodhráns of different shapes and sizes, with and without skin decoration. The laminated playing sticks are made by Dave Harper.

timbers before they are turned on the lathe. As well as looking very pretty, they are also well balanced, and Paraic described them as all made from 'good heavy hardwood'. Not surprisingly, they are also rather expensive.

Paraic still travels to different fleadhanna; nowadays to sell his instruments, and for this purpose he has a trailer which converts into a mobile Bodhrán shop. When I met him at the fleadh in Enniscorthy (2000), he had a stall beside Gerry Bourke, another instrument maker. Gerry travels quite a lot, and he also sells some of Paraic McNeela's Bodhráns; notably the tunable models. In his own craft Gerry concentrates on light-weight learners' instruments. Introductory Bodhrán lessons are included in the sale of his instruments and, like Eamon Maguire, he takes time to talk to his customers. More importantly, he also includes some advice on social considerations in session playing, as in the excitement of a fleadh it is all too easy for novice Bodhrán players to follow a sudden urge to try out their new instrument with other musicians. All too often in the past this has caused problems for experienced session musicians, and an important thing the novice has to learn is to know when *not* to play the Bodhrán. Or, as Ciaran Carson has worded it:

FIG. 1.33:

Instrument maker Gerry Bourke travels professionally to sell his own and Paraic McNeela's Bodhráns. Like other instrument makers, he provides instructions about playing and care to his customers, especially if they are newcomers to the Bodhrán.

Familiarise yourself as thoroughly as possible with the music before approaching within smelling distance of a goat-skin… If you want to join a session, ask the other musicians first, or wait until you are asked. This common courtesy should be observed by all musicians, but bodhrán players seem to ignore it more than most. (Carson 1986:38–9)

Needless to say, the only way to learn social behaviour is through experience. Every musician is different, and sometimes indeed the opposite problem arises. Gill (Sharon Gillespie), a Belfast session musician, recounts that when she first started playing the Bodhrán in public, the other musicians – who were actually looking for a Bodhrán player – had to encourage her a few times; first to play at all, and then to play a bit louder. So Carson's advice may need to be modified, depending on the specific conditions.

James Davey (Sonny Davey) from Killavil, Co. Sligo, who is by now in his nineties, comes from a farming background, and he is one of the best-known instrument makers of the older generation. The name 'Sonny' is a pet name which was given to him as a child. James does not actually *make* Bodhráns any longer, as he feels that he should enjoy the later years of his life with his children – three sons and three daughters – and his

FIG. 1.34:
Instrument maker
James (Sonny) Davey

grandchildren. He describes all of his children as musical, and he relates that they all would play music together at his house from time to time: 'They do come sometimes here, and I have the drums out… and we do have a great session – some music, you know? It brightens things up so well. And they're a terribly good family to me.'

His grandchildren are interested in music as well, and two of them – Aisling and Stephen – sang and danced for me while I was visiting (and I played them some tunes in return). Apart from full-size instruments, James has also made some smaller Bodhráns, for children to learn to play the instrument.

FIG. 1.35:

Apart from full-size instruments, James Davey has made a number of smaller-size instruments for the use of children. Here he looks on as his grandson Stephen gives the instrument a careful tinkle.

I asked James how he had started off his craft, and he told me this story, which took place around 1920:

> When I started making Bodhráns first, there was an old flute player who lived only across the fields from here, and he made a little Bodhrán; it was a sand screen. And I went out at all the crossroads with him, hitting that little Bodhrán. He was a flute player. But I was chastised for not been doing me lessons, so I had to finish at that. But I was in a hall in Bunanadden and we were having a tune. And there was a man there, who was Matt Mulholland. He was a step dancer; he was from Sligo town. I think his family is there too. And he came over and he said to me, 'I wonder where would I get one of those?' I sort of didn't want to tell him, because I was making them for nothing for the people I knew. But I said then that I'd make him a new one. So he took out a wallet and notes out of his pocket, and he said, 'I might as well pay you now, before you make it'. And he counted 'one, two, three, four', and I said 'that's plenty

now'. So that was my first four pound to make a Bodhrán. And I continued the Bodhrán... And when my name was round about for a lot then I got money from several people telling me to make a Bodhrán for them. And they told me if it was more [money] they'd give me more. So I continued like that. And it was good.

The official start of James' craft business took place in 1927, by which time he had organised himself a workshop space to work in. During the early days the Daveys had the tourist trade in mind, and some of James' early instruments carried the inscription 'Souvenir of Ireland'. But these early days did not last long, and as his instruments acquired a reputation among musicians in Ireland, James started to develop his individual style of Bodhrán construction.

James is one of the instrument makers who gave all his Bodhráns a personal mark in appearance, which identifies them as his instruments. The rims of his drums are painted in a yellowy-brownish colour, and they carry two bands of decoration around the rim: one which secures the skin to the rim with upholstery nails, and another band attached around the opposite side of the rim (See colour plate 8 on page xix). Exactly the same features show on small instruments, which James has made for children.

In addition to these features his Bodhráns can easily be identified by their skins, as these always carry a stamp with his name and address on their inside. James told me that the standard size of his heads was 15 inches. The frame is constructed from two layers of plywood, and James said that he always made his rims to a width of 3 1/2 inches. Nowadays, this is considered rather a narrow width for frames, but James Davey's influence shows, for instance, in instruments produced by the Roundstone, Co. Galway, Bodhrán maker Malachy Kearns.

James relates that he used to get his skins from the local farmers, who sometimes wanted to get rid of their goats if they interfered with their cattle. But the best skins of all, he thinks, come from mountain goats: 'Occasionally you would get a wild goat, but they are very hard to catch. Mountain goats were always the best. I found that there was a better skin on them. It came out a better tone all the time.' James said he always used the same method to cure his skins: just ordinary lime and water. The skins are left in a barrel of lime solution and held down by a weight. He would leave them there for ten to twelve days, or maybe two weeks, depending on the individual skins, by which time the hair would come off easily.

FIG. 1.36:
In playing the
Bodhrán, James Davey
attaches the stick with
an elastic band to his
middle finger. This is a
not-so-common
playing style, but it is
not restricted to any
particular region.

David G. Such, who spoke to James Davey in the early 1980s – when James was still making Bodhráns – describes how James would tack the bare and damp skins onto a board and leave them to dry thoroughly for three to six months, before he would use them to make a Bodhrán. The skins were then soaked for about an hour, and using a string as an aid, he tied the skins to the rim in the process of tightening the drum head over the frame (Such 1985:14). During the early 1930s James played in a ceili band. Inspired by the morning sun rising up over the mountains when they came home from a late night of playing music, they called their band 'The Rising Sun Ceili Band', and James made all the drums for the band.

Throughout his Bodhrán-making career, James would always strive for the highest quality, and he told me that he gave a guarantee to his customers to re-skin the instruments without charge if the skins should prove faulty. Some customers seem to have misunderstood this idea, as James relates:

> There was a doctor from Lanesborough [Co. Longford]. He came down to a place we used to play there, and he said to me, 'Aren't you the Bodhrán maker?' I said 'I am.' And he said, 'Well, you have to re-bottom my Bodhrán for me.' And I said, 'What's wrong?' And he said, 'I was going out to the toilet, and I left down the Bodhrán at the seat, and someone threw a butt of a cigarette into it. And it burned a hole in the bottom of it.'

Through the Davey family's laughter, which followed, I gathered that James then gave him 'a wee lecture' on what the guarantee did *not* cover.

Malachy Kearns – also known as 'Malachy Bodhrán' – has set up his craft business in Roundstone, Co. Galway in Connemara, one of the most beautiful areas in Ireland. Malachy, originally from Dublin, describes himself as having started making Bodhráns in 1976, and as having been taught extensively by the famous musician Peadar Mercier and by the Kerry instrument maker Davy Gunn (deceased) from Duagh outside Listowel (Kearns 1996:24).

At present, Malachy Kearns is probably the best-known Bodhrán maker, as he and his wife Anne – and a number of their helpers – produce instruments for all sections of the market; including the tourist trade. Anne Kearns, who is responsible for the skin decorations, specialises in family crests, but she also does traditional designs. Other designs can be produced on request. Their music and craft shop is well known among tourists from all over the world, and it is indeed regularly frequented by visitors from various different nations. Marty, an American visitor to the shop kindly presented his new Bodhrán for me, which he had just acquired in August 2000 (see Fig. 1.37 on page 34). The music shop sells instruments from many world cultures, and is housed in the same building as the craft shop, where a wide variety of items can be obtained – such as little woolly sheep, keyrings, tea towels, and wickerwork baskets. The music shop also sells videos, tapes, CDs, and printed music, and it includes a section of second-hand instruments. There is also a large variety of playing sticks on sale. At the back of the shop a video instructs visitors on how to play the Bodhrán, and behind a glass screen a number of helpers can be observed in the workshop, occupied with the processes of instrument construction.

FIG. 1.37:
Marty, an American
visitor, presents his
Bodhrán, newly
purchased from
Malachy Kearns'
Roundstone music
shop.

Opposite
FIG. 1.38:
Irish emigrant
children on a home
visit display their newly
acquired Roundstone
instruments outside
Roundstone village.

FIG. 1.39:
James O'Donovan
uses a rounded zigzag
pattern and a double
row of upholstery nails
to attach his skins to
the frame.

Kearns' Bodhráns vary widely in size, shape, and quality – catering for very different tastes and requirements. Not surprisingly, a large section is taken up by lightweight learners' instruments with 16 and 18 inch heads and rather shallow rims (around 3 to 3 1/2 inches wide). Some of these instruments vividly bring to mind the origins of the Bodhrán as a household implement – e.g. a tray for storing and serving food – except that Kearns' instruments carry pretty skin decorations. The tunable models steeply rise in price, and they are fitted with five tuning pegs. Some rims are made from steamed hardwoods, such as ash, beech, or birch (Kearns 1996:20). There is also a large section of children's size instruments available. They may be bought sometimes as souvenirs (Kearns 1996:21), but there are also keyring-size Bodhráns available, about 3 inches in diameter, and I was told that they are made from a bamboo-like hollow timber.

As it is impossible to discuss *all* instrument makers in detail, I will end this section by giving a few more examples of instrument makers whose Bodhráns can be identified by particular marks.

James O'Donovan, a Tipperary instrument maker, who was also influenced by Charlie Byrne, produces Bodhráns, that show a decorative rounded zig-zag pattern along the edges of the skin. This particular instrument was made in the 1970s, and belongs to Breda Donnelly from Enniscorthy. Breda told me that in the old days 'they had their Bodhrán hung in the hall', and in the morning they 'would tap it, in order to get information about the weather'.

Nowadays, Bodhráns are not only made in Ireland. Roddy Turner from the south of England, for instance, produces distinctive instruments with frames decorated with handcrafted inlay work of differently-coloured timbers. Not surprisingly, they

FIG. 1.40:
Walton's of Dublin
use a special process to
transfer decorative
ornaments to their
skins.

are rather expensive, as the processes involved in their construction are time-consuming and require an extra amount of work.

In Sheffield, England, Brian Howard makes Bodhráns, for which he uses Remo fibre skins. These skins have the distinct advantage of not being affected by air moisture, and so they retain their tuning in all weather conditions. They produce a warm and mellow sound, which certainly resembles the traditional timbre of the instrument. There are also tunable models available, for specific pitch requirements. Remo Belli is, of course, the world's best-known producer of percussion instruments. According to Eric Cunningham's information Remo have also produced Bodhráns themselves, for which 'until recently they used fibreskin heads, but now use Reemlar, a treated Mylar head that they market under the name Legacy' (Cunningham 1999:17).

Another well-known source of high quality Bodhráns is Walton's in Dublin. Their drums are made by different instrument makers to specific instructions, but they are also easily recognisable. Walton's use a screen-printing process to transfer decorations onto their skins. This gives their drums a very neat and bright appearance.

Comparison of the construction processes of both drums

When examining the construction processes of the Lambeg and the Bodhrán in comparison, it becomes obvious that both drums have a lot in common as far as materials are concerned, but that these materials are worked in completely different ways. These different processes are related to the diametrically opposed sound qualities which are expected of the two instruments. While the Lambeg is desired to give a high-pitched ringing sound, the Bodhrán is expected to produce a low-pitched sound which is further damped in playing. An exception are Séamus O'Kane's Bodhráns, which are made from Lambeg skins and therefore represent a cross-over form of instrument.

The obvious explanation that would suggest itself would be to ascribe these expected different sound qualities to the sizes of the drums. But historical processes show that, although both instruments have changed their sizes over time, their desired sound qualities were essentially the same as nowadays. This indicates that changes in their construction moved in harmony with cultural expectations, and that these merely served to reinforce the characteristic timbral properties of the two drums. These essential sound qualities are mainly achieved through the different treatments of the skins.

The timbers used in the construction of the body/frame of the two drums do not vary essentially either, although the Bodhrán is considerably more flexible, as the frame only plays a minimal part in the sound amplification of the instrument. As far as the Lambeg is concerned, considerable pressures are working on various parts of the instrument. The Lambeg therefore requires solid timber in its construction, which needs to be steamed for turning. But many Bodhrán makers produce instruments from layered plywood as well as from solid timbers, including oak.

An interesting social aspect is that, although Lambegs and Bodhráns produced nowadays in Ireland are of an extremely high technological standard in their construction, most instrument makers do not see their craft as a profession – or at least not as a full-time profession. Of course there are exceptions, but many instrument makers come from a woodworking background, and they tend to see drum making rather as a 'special hobby' that has emerged from their

FIG. 1.41:
Like many Lambeg makers, Frank Orr, seen here outside his workshop, lives in a rural area, which provides sufficient space for comfortable instrument construction.

knowledge of working with timber. But it is certainly a rather prestigious 'hobby', much respected within their communities and indeed far beyond.

Especially in Lambeg crafting, a lot of work involves not so much the making of drums, but the restoration of valuable old instruments. Individual drums have individual histories attached to them, and they are given individual names (see Chapter 4). The repair and maintenance of these old instruments requires skill, adaptation concerning aspects of technology, a historical knowledge on the construction of the instruments, and a good amount of idealism. Richard Sterritt showed me an old drum shell he was working on. It was cracked in many places and required lots of patient work of carefully widening up the gaps to clean them thoroughly, and then to glue them together again. And Richard's brother Roly provided the socio-cultural explanation: 'It would be easier to make a new drum, but it is a sin to see one dying. We're trying to revive it with a kiss of life'. Bodhrán makers also take care in repairing valuable old instruments, but they tend to use less flowery language, and they do not ascribe individual names to instruments. Rather, the drums are referred to just by the name of the instrument maker.

The craft of instrument construction for both drums requires a

FIG. 1.42:
Many instrument
makers from the older
generation – like
Charlie Byrne – used
to work from home.

sufficiently large work space. In the case of Lambeg drums this will
be at least a medium-sized workshop, as instrument parts and the
steaming equipment are of fairly large dimensions. Most Lambeg
makers live in rural areas, and have their workshops in sheds in the
immediate vicinity of their houses. The older generation of Bodhrán
makers also usually had their workspaces attached to – or in close
proximity to – their houses. Often their workshop would be a shed
in the yard, so that they would be working from home as well.

FIG. 1.43:
Malachy Kearns' music
shop is located in a
modern craft centre,
which caters for various
different demands of
the market.

In recent times, and particularly in urban areas, Bodhrán makers have taken to setting up separate workshops, with more or less regular working hours. Once Bodhrán making becomes a full-time occupation – as it has nowadays with a number of instrument makers – working 'from home' becomes impractical, as larger working spaces are required. This also has implications for the social life in the community, as instrument makers' workshops often develop into meeting places for local and visiting musicians, and occasionally one can come across spontaneous performances of the most interesting and highest quality music.

2
The use of the drums within society

Music can express social attitudes and cognitive processes,
but it is useful and effective only when it is heard by the
prepared and receptive ears of people who have shared,
or can share in some way, the cultural and individual
experiences of its creators.

John Blacking 1976:54

There lies no inherent meaning in a particular musical sound or instrument; such meanings are culture-specific, and they are socially constructed. Also, no music is performed in a social vacuum; it is performed by people (musicians) and for people (an audience), although there may be an overlap between both categories. The meaning of particular musical sounds and instruments derives from a shared consensus between groups of people. The meaning of a particular piece of music may change considerably, depending on its immediate performance context. An example would be an identical performance of a particular country's national anthem in different countries, and/or at different social events. Under certain social conditions the musically identical performance can even act as a parody.

This chapter looks at the different social contexts in which the Lambeg and the Bodhrán are played in Ireland nowadays. It should be borne in mind, that one layer of meaning derives from shared western culture, which ascribes military associations to drums in general. Further, drums, within western cultures may be perceived as secular musical instruments; as commercial commodities, which can be bought and sold at a particular market value. Of course, these common, shared ascriptions of meanings in western culture do not preclude further – or deeper – layers of meaning being associated with particular musical instruments or performance contexts.

Either way these socially constructed meanings are not clear-cut, and they will vary not only from event to event, but also between groups of people and indeed between different individuals. My purpose in this chapter is not so much to give an interpretation of these socially constructed meanings, but rather to describe the social contexts where the drums are used within present-day society.

The Lambeg
Parades

Not everyone in society sees drums as musical instruments. When I asked a young lady on the upper Ormeau Road in Belfast on the morning of the Twelfth of July (2000) when the parade would be coming down the road, she replied, 'I don't know. When you hear the banging you know they are here'. I am quoting this example because the terminology of 'banging' is symptomatic of our society in relation to drums, no matter how complicated playing styles may be performed on the instruments. It is an indication that symbolic perceptions of drums in our society are more widespread than musical perceptions.

On the other side of the Ormeau bridge – along the lower Ormeau Road – such musical perception is also widely lacking. Tensions have arisen in connection with these marches, and it is therefore hardly surprising that people's attention is not particularly focused on the musical qualitites of the drum. Opinions about these parades vary widely within present-day society: while at one end of the spectrum they are described as happy carnivalesque events with deep traditional roots, at the other end of the spectrum they are seen as out-of-date rituals which support unequal power structures in society and cause disturbances for the every-day life of people. There are various shades of opinions between these two extreme points. There are a number of excellent anthropological studies available (eg Cecil 1993, Buckley and Kenney 1995, Buckley 1998, Jarman 1999), which focus on the use of paraphernalia in marching contexts as identity markers. I do not intend to add to this body of literature, as my interest lies in the musical roles of the drums within society.

In most of the musical performances at present-day parades the bass drum provides a basic rhythm, which usually emphasises the first and third beats of each bar. Against this simple, steady rhythm of the bass drum will be set the syncopated rhythms of the side drums. These present-day rhythms are a far cry from the traditional styles performed by Lambeg drums to accompany the fife in the processions around the Twelfth of July in previous times. Nowadays Lambeg drums are rarely – and only in some rural areas – seen within marching contexts. Most drums are privately owned today, and many drummers are reluctant to have their valuable instruments used within marching contexts. This book concentrates on the musical role of the two traditional drums in Ireland, but readers who are interested in present-day parading practices, marching band culture and paraphernalia used within these contexts are referred to Neil Jarman (2000) or Dominic Bryan (2000, esp pp.143–7).

The large drum included in present-day marching bands will be the bass drum, which is about half the size of a Lambeg drum. This makes it a lot easier for the drummers to carry their instruments in processions. For an illustration of the use of bass drums in present-day parades see colour plate 9 on page xix.

This changeover to the use of the smaller drum seems to have been the long-term result of the speeding up of rhythms, which took place during the early decades of the twentieth century. In her work on the Lambeg drum Fionnuala Scullion mentions that it is said that at around this time Lambeg drummers were actually banned from the Belfast procession, as they were regarded as holding back the march by walking too slowly (Scullion 1981:23). During my research I have also heard such references being made within the drumming community.

Walking for miles while playing a heavy drum which hangs from the neck of the musician seems indeed a rather strenuous exercise, which cannot be carried out beyond a certain speed. It remains open to debate whether the inclusion of brass instruments in marches during the early decades of the twentieth century led to a speeding up of the rhythms, or whether the increased speed necessitated a change in instrumentation. Either way, within marching contexts the Lambeg drum nowadays seems to hold only a historically grounded iconographic status, which is preserved rather in people's minds than on the road. To see and hear the playing of Lambeg drums today, one most likely will have to go to one of the competitions, which are held – usually on Saturdays – at various locations all over Northern Ireland.

Competitions

Nowadays, Lambeg drumming competitions are the contexts where playing skills, as well as the related folk myths and lore, are preserved and developed. Fionnuala Scullion (1981:25) explains that these drumming competitions have developed from the pre-war contexts of 'stick-ins', where two drummers in opposition challenged each other's strength and endurance by performing competing rhythms, sometimes for many long hours. An important aspect, which has transferred from these historical performance contexts, is that these events serve to bring together people from different areas, who are interested in Lambeg drumming culture. Otherwise, present-day drumming competitions are rather different events, and it is worth taking a detailed look at such an event.

Smaller competitions – with maybe around twelve drums/drummers – take place almost every Saturday, except for a period of about two months around Christmas. But there are a few major events, which attract fifty to sixty drums/drummers. One of these major competitions takes place annually at the last Saturday in July in Markethill, Co. Armagh.

In 2000 the event had to cope with frequently and rapidly changing weather conditions. The afternoon was pleasant and mostly dry, and drums began to arrive in Markethill from around 3.45pm. People were drawing nearer from different directions, and as the drums were played on their approach to the central market square, you could hear the individual sounds coming closer from different sides. The drummers then made for one or another of the local pubs around the market square, but the drums were brought out again every now and then for another demonstration. People gathered to listen to these demonstrations, but the competition proper did not start until around 7pm.

During the evening the proceedings were frequently delayed because of sudden showers, and the drummers' fear of breaking their drum heads was very obvious, as the drums were immediately taken into the local pubs as soon as the first raindrops fell. Nevertheless

spirits remained high, as the frequent breaks allowed for plenty of socialising. Also present in Markethill was a television team from BBC Northern Ireland, who were filming material for Ian Kirk-Smith's documentary on the Lambeg drum, which looks at Lambeg-and-fife performances as well as at competition drumming. It also mentions historical aspects of the different performance contexts.[1]

For the competition procedure labels with numbers are attached to the drums, and then each drum is paraded up to where the judges are waiting. Depending on the importance of the event, there may be two to five judges, and additionally there is a 'marker' present, who writes up the score. Before the drums are taken up to the judges, a final knocking and pulling is applied to the drum by the drummer's company, as volume, pitch and tone will be assessed as well as the equal balancing of sound between the two drum heads. There will be three rounds for the drums to be paraded before the judges, and in each round the drum needs to be awarded full points by all judges in order to proceed into the next round. In the first round each judge can award 10 points to the drum, and in the second, 20 points. In the third round the drums are placed in order of preference. The

FIG. 2.1:

Lambeg drummers line up to parade their drums before the judges of a competition. The composition of musicians and spectators at these events is mostly male.

[1] Part 2 (The Lambeg Drum) of a four-part series on musical traditions in Northern Ireland, produced and directed by Ian Kirk-Smith, first shown on BBC 2 (TV) in March 2001.

winning drum receives a cup, and in addition there will be some
small money prizes. At major events – such as Markethill – there may
be as many as twenty prizes, but their monetary values are merely
symbolic. The first drum may win a prize of £50, and the other winners will receive prizes between £15 and £5. This would, of course,
hardly pay for the drummers' travelling expenses to take part in the
competition.

Taking part seems to be considerably more important than winning, except for the prestige value gained for the drum. This distribution of emphasis seems to be confirmed by the fact that there are
no agreed standards as to how to judge the drums. In response to my
inquiries as to what would be considered 'the best sound' I was told
that some judges like 'an old baggy sound', while others will prefer 'a
musical drum with a high pitch and a sparkle', and yet others may
like 'just a musical sound'.

Indeed, varied language is employed to explain differences in the
sounds of different drums. Fionnuala Scullion (1981:28) quotes the
historical Belfast Lambeg maker William Hewitt as giving the following description:

> ... till the uninitiated ear... they are all the same... But when I go
> out and I hear ten Lambeg drums there's not two of them drums
> drummed the same. Even if there was eighty Lambeg drums there's

not two of them drummed the same... There's such variation... Out of a drum you get tone, weight and bit of steel forby and quickness you see... you get different combinations... You get a drum there that's very very light in tone and then you get a drum that's heavy toned, but in between that you get maybe forty drums that their tone is different from the lowest toned drums to the highest tone drum... And you get a toney drum that's slow and you get a toney drum that's quick and... steely forby tone, then you get another drum that's toney and quick and no steel.

One aspect that differs essentially from Bodhrán competitions is that it is not so much the skill of the drummer but the sound of the drum itself, which is assessed in Lambeg competitions. Of course the drumming skills of the musicians will be essential for bringing out this sound, and indeed the groups which bring a drum to a competition will choose their drummers carefully. But they will make their choices according to whom they consider most suited to bring out the sounds of the drum, as the general attention at competitions is focused on the sound of the instruments.

FIG. 2.3:

Junior Tweedie, a spectator at the Markethill competition 2000, is making sure to start learning his rhythms in time.

A side effect of this focus on the sound qualities of the drums – as opposed to the playing skills of individual drummers – has been that a lot of the old traditional tunes for the Lambeg-and-fife have been neglected, as the old repertoire held no particular relevance in the context of present-day drumming competitions. According to Gary Hastings (personal communication), especially at competitions, many people are nowadays just improvising on the basic rhythms of

2/4, 4/4 and 3/4. This may well be the case in some competitions, as in any musical genre one will find master musicians as well as learners. But improvisation can only take place when people have a musical frame to improvise to. The experienced Lambeg drummers I spoke to were using set patterns, to which they improvise the ornamentation, which is itself governed by structural considerations.

The reason why people nevertheless refer to 'tunes' of the Lambeg is that there is a double meaning attached to the word 'tune' within Lambeg drumming circles. Fionnuala Scullion has pointed out that when a drummer is referred to as 'only having one tune', it can mean that he can only drum in one style (Scullion 1981:29). The modern concept of Lambeg 'tunes' seems to be an extension of this idea, which now appears to encompass a mixture of style, rhythm, time, and actual tune structure (in the sense of a melody being associated with the drumming part). It may, for instance, indicate a particular drumming pattern, which individual musicians have learnt from each other. When drummers therefore declare that they play various 'tunes', they are not 'bluffing', as they are not necessarily implying that they know a variety of traditional Lambeg-and-fife tunes. They are merely using the convention of terminology used within Lambeg drumming circles.

Another striking difference – not just to Bodhrán competitions, but also to similar events like country fairs or community festivals – is the gender composition at Lambeg drumming events. As I point out at different points in this book – and from different angles – there are various cultural reasons why Lambeg drumming is considered to be a male activity. These gender associations are reflected in the composition of spectators at Lambeg competitions. This does not mean that there are no women present at these events, but at present they are certainly a small minority.

A brave pioneer in Lambeg drumming circles is Caroline Stewart from Armagh, whom I first met at the Markethill competition. Twenty-year-old Caroline took up playing the drum about five years ago, and since then she has resolutely ventured into the male world of Lambeg competitions. Caroline can look back on a few generations of Stewarts with an interest in Lambeg drumming, and she thinks that playing the Lambeg should not be an exclusively male domain at all. Caroline's experiences in the male dominated contexts of drumming matches are discussed in more detail in Chapter 5.

FIG. 2.4:
Caroline Stewart from Armagh is at present the only female Lambeg drummer taking part in competitions.

Eleventh-night drumming

All over Northern Ireland it is customary to hold celebrations on the Eleventh-Night, which precedes the Twelfth of July parades. In many places bonfires are lit, and often children collect the timber for these bonfires. In rural areas the celebrations may be held on top of a hill, and a brazier – filled with sticks and oil – may be erected to roast chestnuts. In some rural areas Lambeg drumming will take place at these bonfires, and there are also a few places where only Lambeg drumming takes place – without a bonfire. Loughgall village in Co. Armagh used to have a drumming-only tradition, but the experienced drummer who used to lead the procession has since died.

It is regarded as an honour to be asked to take part in these processions, and only well qualified drummers will be asked to do so. The playing style will be single-time or double-time, and the repertoire will be the same as the one used in competitions. Depending on the area, the drummers use their own regional 'dialects' to interpret this repertoire. The stylistic details are discussed below in Chapter 3. For people not familiar with the aesthetic significance of the Lambeg to its practitioners, the sound of such midnightly drumming can evoke eerie associations. The drumming is perceived by some as carrying a sense of sectarian menace and as 'establishing territorial claims'. The latter aspect can be interpreted locally, regionally, or nationally. For discussions of social interpretations of Lambeg drumming I refer the interested reader to the relevant anthropological literature (e.g. Buckley and Kenney 1995). This book focuses on the musical role of the drums.

The Bodhrán

Parades

Although the Bodhrán has in recent decades assumed certain symbolism as an instrument associated with the nationalist Irish tradition, it is rarely – if ever – found in nationalist marching contexts. The occasional Bodhrán may be found as a visual object displaying nationalist symbolism, but within present-day marching contexts the Bodhrán is normally not used as a musical instrument. This is not surprising, as the volume of Bodhráns is easily drowned out within marching contexts. The drum which was found within nationalist marching contexts until fairly recently was indeed the Lambeg drum. Nationalist symbolism could be found in the decoration of the drums associated with the Ancient Order of Hibernians (AOH), and details of these instruments are discussed in Chapter 4. For some decorated Hibernian drums see colour plates 4 and 5 on page xvii. But there is also a plainshell Hibernian drum in existence, which is nowadays used in drumming matches. It is known as 'The Banbrook Plainshell'.

The only time the Bodhrán is found in parading contexts is during the processions of the 'Wren Boys', which are discussed in detail in Chapter 4. Here often a number of Bodhráns are found, and they play the basic rhythm in unison. Kevin Danaher describes that on a quiet day in the country the sound of the Bodhrán in such processions may be heard for a mile or more (Danaher 1955:129). This is, of course, still much less than the volume of a Lambeg drum heard playing in the countryside.

Community Settings

Nowadays, the most frequent contexts where the Bodhrán is heard are community events where traditional Irish music is performed. Here the Bodhrán is used as a percussive accompanying instrument, which underlines and accentuates the various melody instruments played in these contexts. Such events may be staged performances or informal community sessions. In either of these settings it is unusual for more than one Bodhrán to be played at a time, as the simultaneous playing of two or more Bodhráns is culturally perceived as undesirable: it is said that either their 'rhythms clash', or that their volume will be 'too overpowering'. If on occasion one finds two Bodhráns being played simultaneously, it is most likely that the two musicians know each other well and have worked out stylistic details in relation to each other. Ultimately cultural acceptance will depend on the status of the participating musicians – and generally within the range of status ascriptions to musical instruments, the Bodhrán will be found at the lower end of the spectrum. This hierarchical concept of status ascription to the rhythm section within traditional

FIG. 2.5:

Traditional music sessions – like this one at Queen's University Belfast – take place regularly at various small venues all over Ireland. The Bodhrán player in the picture is Gill (Sharon) Gillespie from Belfast.

music coincides largely with status ascriptions within the western art music tradition. It is likely that these value judgements have been transferred within society from one musical genre to the other.

Competitions

FIG. 2.6:

The annual competitions held at fleadhanna are organised by Comhaltas Ceoltóirí Éireann. The Bodhrán player in the picture is Eamon Murray from Loughbeg, Co. Antrim, who was the winner of the All-Ireland-Fleadh 2000 in the 12-to-15-years age group.

The events where the Bodhrán can be found in competition contexts are the annual fleadhanna organised by Comhaltas Ceoltóirí Éireann (CCÉ),[2] which include regional and national events. At these the Bodhrán has now been fully accepted as a traditional instrument, and its playing style has become increasingly sophisticated over the last few years.

The role of the instrument is seen as complementary to melody instruments, and consequently Bodhrán players will always perform in combination with one or more melody instruments. Their performance will be assessed in relation to how the Bodhrán 'colours the tune of the melody instrument'. Of course it will be important that the player can keep in time with the melody instrument, but the

---

[2] Comhaltas Ceoltóirí Éireann, an organisation established in 1951–52 to promote and support traditional Irish culture. At present, CCÉ has local, regional, and national branches, and in many other countries as well.

Musical competitions take place at the annual Fleadhanna Ceoil organised by CCÉ, also subdivided between county, province, and national level. The most important event is the national-level All-Ireland Fleadh, which takes place in August each year at different locations.

assessors will also look for variation of tone, and how the player uses the capacity of the instrument to achieve these different tones.

A Bodhrán competition is a very sober event. Outside, the community festival may be in full swing, but at competitions you find a concert hall atmosphere. At this year's All-Ireland-Fleadh in Enniscorthy the atmosphere at the competitions was so delicate, that I had to press the release button of my camera very softly, so as not to disturb the performances. To me the quietness of the event was all the more outstanding, as it took place only a few weeks after the Markethill Lambeg competition; and it is certainly also in stark contrast to the atmosphere at informal community music-making events, such as sessions. The assessors at CCÉ competitions are called 'adjudicators' – not 'judges' – and there may be one or two of them at each event. They will give percentage-rated points to each performer, and at the end of each section they will decide on a first, second, and third place. The sections are divided between different age groups (under 12, 12 to 15, 15 to 18, and over 18). The first three winners of each section receive medals, and in some competitions there is also a cup. The latter is a perpetual trophy, which is passed on every year with the name of each winner being added to the trophy. There are no money prizes awarded in these competitions – not even nominal ones – but there is much prestige attached to participation in general, and to winning in particular.

Storytelling, recitations, and the Wren tradition

By far the oldest – and the most traditional – performance contexts of the Bodhrán in Ireland as a musical instrument are the annual folk customs related to the Wren tradition. These took place in various parts of Ireland on 26 December – St Stephen's Day – and their details are discussed in Chapter 4. Prior to the 1960s folk revival, in many parts of Ireland the Bodhrán is reported to have been played only for this one annual occasion (cf. Danaher 1959:669, Vallely 1999:29). The 'Wren Boys' would parade from house to house within their parish, and at each house they performed their dances, songs and recitations. For these they would use one or more Bodhráns, and often also any of a variety of other instruments. In some parts of Ireland – primarily in Kerry – the Wren Boys' annual performances are still practised as a folk tradition. To argue, as some writers do, that the Bodhrán held no importance in Ireland before the 1960s,

FIG. 2.7:

The Armagh Rhymers performing at the Ulster Folk & Transport Museum in Cultra, Co. Down.

A large part of their repertoire is directed towards children, but their performances are equally enjoyed by people from all age groups.

since the Wren Boys' processions took place only once a year, is unsatisfactory. The Bodhrán held a pride of place in these folk customs, and the Wren tradition was indeed very widespread in Ireland (cf. Danaher 1959, 1966).

The Wren Boys' repertoires integrate fragments from different historical periods, and there seems to be a large overlap of repertoire between Wren Boy processions, mummers' plays, and traditional mumming customs at Irish wakes and weddings. Like other mummers, the Wren Boys dress up in costumes, which often include straw and/or willow wickerwork masks, and they use ribbons, tinsel and various other odds and ends as a decoration. Kevin Danaher (1972:244) mentions that according to Patrick Kennedy's description (Banks of the Boro, 233–4) the Wren Boys were historically at the lower end of social esteem among these different mummers' groups. The various myths associated with the custom of 'hunting the wren' are described in Chapter 4.

From the second half of the twentieth century onward the traditional mummers' plays have gained renewed popularity in Ireland.

Instrumental in this growing popularity have been the Armagh Rhymers, a professional group of mummers, who nowadays take their performances to various corners of the world. Apart from giving performances, the Armagh Rhymers do a lot of workshops with children, which by now have been received enthusiastically by successive generations of children. The masks of the Armagh Rhymers are made from willow by John Mulholland from Aughagallon, Co. Antrim.

A similar tradition is carried on by storytellers, who draw on the same musical means of presentation, but on different repertoires. Storytellers do not use any mumming regalia, but many of them make use of a Bodhrán for their presentation. Seventy-year-old Jim O'Connor from Newmarket, Co. Cork, is a storyteller who now lives in Ardfert, Co. Kerry. Jim performs often at local community events, and his repertoire consists of stories, recitations and poems. Some of Jim's repertoire has been passed on to him from his father (also named Jim O'Connor), a sean-nós[3] singer, who also did recitations.

FIG. 2.8:

Traditional mummers costumes are made from materials which have a background history in their community. The ornaments used for decoration will be changed in relation to the annual folk calendar. This photograph was taken at Halloween 2000.

---

[3] Literally 'old style'; a traditional genre of unaccompanied song, which makes use of free rhythmic structures and highly melismatic ornamentation of the melodic line.

But over the years Jim has also added a lot of his own material.

Jim plays an old, battered Davy Gunn[4] Bodhrán, which is decorated with goat's milk stickers, and he uses it to accentuate his stories and recitations. When he performs in pubs he may also use the Bodhrán to 'drum up' attention for telling a story, as the attention of his audience may be scattered at the beginning of a night. In performances Jim uses a variety of playing styles, the combination of which arises from the immediate circumstances. Jim thinks that books teaching the playing of the Bodhrán are of limited use, as he says: 'You cannot really write it down. You have to feel the music. One musician feels one thing, and he plays that. Another musician feels another thing, and he plays that. It depends on what you feel.' For Jim the Bodhrán is an additional means to express his feelings through his performance. This is certainly a concept about music generally held in western culture, and it will be expressed by many musicians – not only those from the Irish tradition.

Jim told me a little story, which captures well the ambiguity of meaning that anthropologists have detected in performances of rituals, and which is so often found in the Irish folk tradition. It is indeed very close to some of the folk myths ascribed to Lambeg drums. The event was described as having taken place at a music session at a local fleadh. In anticipation of a performance Jim was rubbing the skin of his Bodhrán to get it at the right temperature for playing (Jim's instrument was constructed before the invention of 'tunable' Bodhráns). When he was asked by a woman nearby why he was doing this, he replied, 'Oh, the goat loves it!'

Sports events

According to Malachy Kearns (1996:78) Bodhráns are nowadays used as national symbols at sports events, and he describes 'many of his bodhráns' as being 'beaten by internationally famed Irish soccer supporters and other sports enthusiasts' (Kearns 1996:19,36). These contexts may well provide an interesting topic for future anthropological studies of the use of musical instruments as national emblems or badges for identity constructions. In the context of this book I am focusing on musical performances of the drums, but symbolic ascriptions of meanings are discussed in Chapters 4 and 5.

---

[4] Davy Gunn is a historical Bodhrán maker from the Listowel area, Co. Kerry.

Other drums used within traditional contexts

Although the Lambeg and the Bodhrán are the only culture-specific traditional drums used in Ireland, there are a few other drums being played within traditional contexts. As described above, at the annual parades associated with the Twelfth of July, you will not only find the bass drum, but also a number of side drums/snare drums, which also have their origin in the European military tradition. The same combination of bass drum and snare drum is found as an accompaniment to ceili band music. Here the two drums are combined with the woodblock, and they are played in the same way as a standard European drum kit would be played; i.e. the musician sits behind the drum kit while he/she plays the woodblock and the snare drum with two drum sticks, and the bass drum is played by a foot mechanism.

During recent years some frame drums of other cultural origins have been played at music sessions. These drums closely resemble the Bodhrán, and they come most often from India, Pakistan, or northern Africa. If such drums – as, for instance, the *bendir* – carry snares, the musicians remove them and they play these drums in the same style as the Bodhrán. Other types of drums are at present only used in stage performances, which value a cross-cultural component in their music, but they do not have any background in Irish community traditions.

FIG. 2.9:
Drummer Eimer Colwell, with Caoimhe Brady (accordion), Darina Brady (flute), and Karlos Brady (banjo), rehearsing in the car park before a competition at the All-Ireland-Fleadh 2000 in Enniscorthy.

Comparison of the performance contexts of the Lambeg and the Bodhrán

Although both the Lambeg and the Bodhrán are used within traditional contexts at community events, there is a marked difference between the cultural associations attached to these performances. While the Lambeg has at present mostly disappeared from marching contexts, the Bodhrán is nowadays mainly associated with community performances of traditional dance music.

Nowadays, the traditional contexts for the Lambeg are the drumming competitions. Here old styles mingle with new, and the traditional lore about the instruments is passed on between the drummers and their community of drumming enthusiasts. People meet to socialise, and the events carry the flair of merry community festivals or country fairs. For the Bodhrán, on the other hand, competitions are only a small component within the range of their uses in community contexts. Socialising and merrymaking take place at fleadhanna, but they are kept outside the halls of the competition proper. Celebrations take place after the competitions are over, and at fleadhanna also a lot of informal music sessions take place; such as those where the Bodhrán is most widely found nowadays within local community contexts. Storytellers, mummers, or other rhymers, who also make use of the Bodhrán, are as likely to be found at fleadhanna as within any other community contexts; such as fairs, festivals, local pubs or clubs.

During recent years some innovative events have taken place – mostly in the form of community workshops – which have tried to integrate the Lambeg as well as the Bodhrán into their performances. Best known of these are the group Different Drums (with Roy Arbuckle and Stephen Matier), and Willie Drennan. Although the stark timbral contrast between the two drums makes them indeed suited for such a combination, the obvious problem results from their extreme differences in volume. A simultaneous performance of both drums will therefore tend to rely on amplification, to level out their differences in volume. This makes it highly unlikely that a community tradition will develop in Ireland which integrates both drums – unless both instruments essentially alter their playing styles and modify their sound qualities.

3
The playing of the drums

In piping and blowing, in plucking and bowing
You can hear the old longing when the music starts,
And the drums are playing; hear what they're saying:
The heartbeat is strong from the love in our hearts.

   written by the author for a radio broadcast, 1996

This chapter takes a comparative look at the playing styles of the Lambeg and the Bodhrán. Playing styles are very culture-specific, and a broad ethnomusicological approach like Alan Lomax's 'Cantometrics' profile.[1] does not yield much information concerning the playing styles discussed in this chapter. The only 'cantometric' information one could draw from this approach is that there is a difference in volume between the two instruments (the Lambeg is considerably louder), that both instruments adhere to a regular metre (which is a general feature of western music), and that the Lambeg is now used as a solo instrument, while the Bodhrán is played in group context.

This last point applies only to the actual performance, and it is not particularly helpful in this context, as a performance constitutes a form of communication between musicians and audiences. In this sense both instruments are played in group contexts, and additionally Lambegs are occasionally played by a pair (or more) of

1 'Cantometrics' was an attempt by the American ethnomusicologist Alan Lomax to show a world-wide relationship between folk song styles and social structure within societies. Of course, folk songs vary widely within societies, making it impossible to collect 'representative' samples. But his model for analysis provides a useful tool for comparing a range of different aspects in musical performances.

FIG. 3.1:
Davy Simpson from Moneymore (right) and Robin Beck from Loughbrickland (back) are getting their drums ready for a competition. The tuning requires a careful balancing between both heads, and it involves tightening the ropes and tapping the hoops with a mallet.

drummers, who coordinate with each other. At most it can be said that the present playing style of the Lambeg has been developed by musicians with a solo performance in mind.

Ethnomusicological studies with a purely organological focus were also not helpful for this section, as they lacked sufficient detail on playing styles, and none of them deal with the specific cultural contexts *and both* instruments I am concerned with. For Bodhrán playing styles I have drawn on a number of short texts from different sources. For Lambeg playing styles I am particularly grateful to Fionnuala Scullion, who carried out her research on the instrument in the 1970s, and who has kindly permitted me to reproduce her detailed musical transcription of a Lambeg-and-fife performance from this period.

The Lambeg

An essential prerequisite for playing the Lambeg drum is the process of tuning its heads. As both heads are connected by means of ropes, which connect their *bracing hoops* and serve to raise or lower the general tension, any change applied to one head will consequently effect the other head. The tuning process therefore requires a good amount of balancing skills. Apart from the *buffs*, which serve to adjust the tension of the ropes, the basic tool used in this procedure is a mallet, to knock the hoops into the desired position. If one of the heads is slack, the procedure of tuning starts by tapping the head and its hoop, and the combination of tapping and knocking serves to balance out the difference between the two heads. As the skins are rather delicately depending on weather conditions, the process of tapping, knocking, and tightening the ropes can take quite a while, until a well-balanced sound concerning timbre, pitch, loudness, and resonance is achieved. In playing, the two heads are struck in rapid alternation between the two sides, and the overall sound effect is supposed to be the same, no matter which way the drum is turned in playing.

Lambeg drummer Caroline Stewart from Armagh told me that the tuning of a drum for playing in a competition actually takes about a week: 'You would pull it a wee bit every day [during the week], and then maybe two or three times on the day of the competition.' Despite its common historical roots and its similarity with the morphological features of the European side drum, the playing style of the latter is rather different from that of the present Lambeg drum.

A pair of identical sticks (described in detail in Chapter 1) is used for playing the Lambeg, and these are essential for achieving what is

Bottom left
FIG. 3.2:
Hand position for playing the Lambeg drum

Bottom right
FIG. 3.3:
Hand position for playing the European side drum

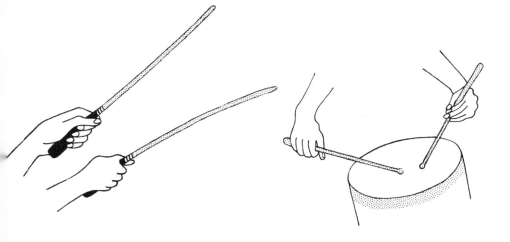

nowadays considered to be a 'good sound'. In playing, the alternation between left-hand and right-hand strokes can reach very high speeds, as triplets and syncopated figures are employed to ornament the performance. Traditional and modern rhymes are used in learning particular drumming patterns – what Lambeg drummers would call a particular 'tune'.

In an interview for a local radio station[2] Roly Sterritt provided an explanation of how the playing style on the Lambeg is constructed. At first a burden text is fixed in the mind – as a mnemonic device – which gives the player the idea of the relation between quavers and crotchets within the particular 'tune' to be performed, such as: 'I think I can drum but I can't'. When beating out the basic rhythm and adding the spoken text, the underlying structure of the 'tune' becomes clear:

FIG. 3.4   **Lambeg learning rhyme 'I think I can drum'**

This basic frame of reference is then further ornamented when being played on the Lambeg:

FIG. 3.5   **Ornamentation of 'I think I can drum'.**

2 Broadcast on Downtown Radio in 1995, in Tommy Sands' weekly two-hour folk music programme 'Country Ceili'.

From the above example it can be seen that the process of ornamentation involves replacing quavers by semiquavers, and this procedure of ornamenting individual notes by means of replacing them by groups of shorter notes – or by adding syncopated variations – requires a skilful handling of the rhythm and of the balancing between left-hand strokes and right-hand strokes by the player. The basic figure used for ornamentation is what Lambeg drummers call 'the roll', and it appears in variations of 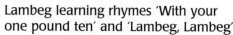 .

Fionnuala Scullion gives a number of other rhymes which were used in the past to help drummers to establish their rhythms. She provides transcriptions of the two best-known ones:

Lambeg learning rhymes 'With your one pound ten' and 'Lambeg, Lambeg' Transcription: Fionnuala Scullion   FIG. 3.6

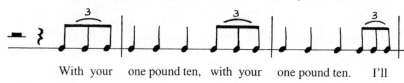

With your   one pound ten, with your   one pound ten.   I'll

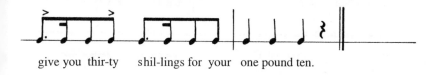

give you thir-ty   shil-lings for your one pound ten.

Lam-beg Lam-beg,   are there any pub – lic hous – es   on the

Lam-beg road Lam – beg.

Richard Sterritt told me that a modern version of the above rhyme would run: 'Lam-beng, diddly-eng deng, diddly-eng deng, are there any public houses on the Lambeg road, diddly-eng deng deng.'

FIG. 3.7:
A Lambeg-and-fife
ensemble from
Ballymena, Co. Antrim,
involving 3 generations
of the Brownlees family.
Photograph by Bobby
Hanvey

Fionnuala Scullion (1982) gives a number of other traditional rhymes, which were used for this purpose: 'Billy McDowell, Billy McDowell, Billy McDowell, Dowell, Dowell' (pron. McDole), or 'Sam McDowell, Billy McDaid, and Old Johnny Jackson', or 'January, February, March, No. April, May, June, No. July, Yes.'[3]

The learning of drumming to rhymes such as these takes place in regional weekly get-togethers, which may sometimes take the form of workshops. In traditional Lambeg styles, an important difference must be pointed out between what is known as 'single-time' drumming and 'double-time' drumming. Single-time drumming is associated with the accompaniment of dance melodies, and it was widely used in the traditional Lambeg-and-fife combination. It is a rather slow style, that makes much use of syncopated figures, such as:

♩♩♩ ♪ ♪ ♩♩♩ or ♫♫ ♫♫ ♫ . Especially in Co. Antrim, single-time drumming is still used in combination with the fife.

Double-time drumming is the style associated with drumming competitions, and it consists of a rather fast and constant beating,

3 A rendition of some of these rhymes to Bodhrán accompaniment (by the Armagh Rhymers) was included in the programme 'A Northern Christmas', produced by Peter Woods for RTÉ Radio 1, broadcast on 26 December 2000. Its main focus is on the Wren tradition.

which is suited for the use of numerous small ornamental rhythmic variations of the individual drummer. The example below was described as a combination of Lambeg styles, showing 'a bit of double and single time floating in and out', and it was performed by the Sterritt brothers.[4]

Example of Lambeg playing
integrating single-time and double-time styles   FIG. 3.8

As I found the example a bit too integrative to recognise the distinguishing marks of the individual styles, I asked the Sterritt family for a more detailed explanation. They gave me an arrangement for a combination of two 'tunes': 'Tandragee Time' in double-time style and 'The Old Sow's Trot to the Perterhole' in single-time style. The piece was performed by Richard Sterritt and his nephew Darren.

4 Broadcast on Downtown Radio in 1995, in Tommy Sands' programme 'Country Ceili'.

In the example Darren starts off playing in double-time, while Richard performs the single-time component. About half-way through the 'tune' (in bar 53) they start changing over, and during the last part of the 'tune' Richard plays the double-time style, while Darren provides the single-time part.

FIG. 3.9: **Arrangement for a combination of different Lambeg drumming styles**

'Tandragee Time' (double-time) and 'The Old Sow's Trot to the Perterhole' (single-time)

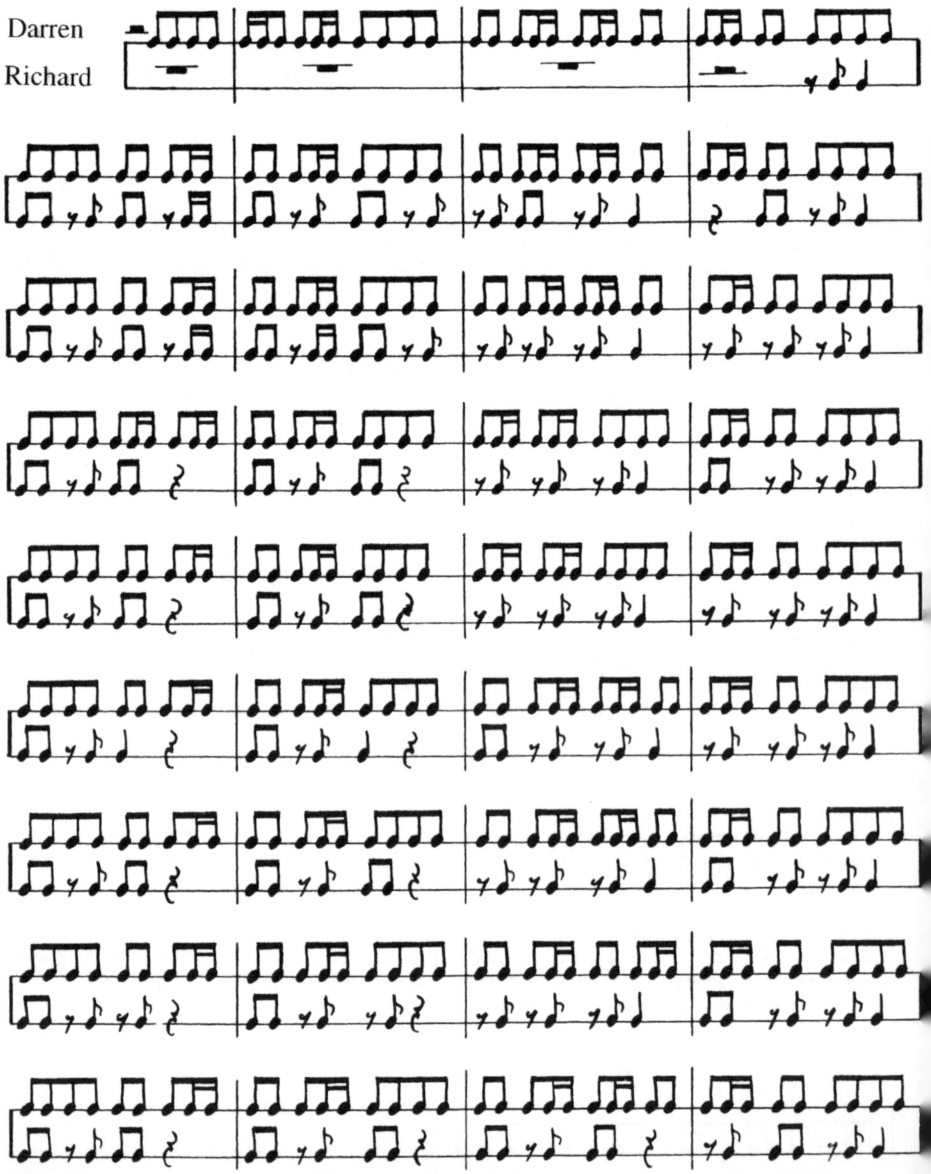

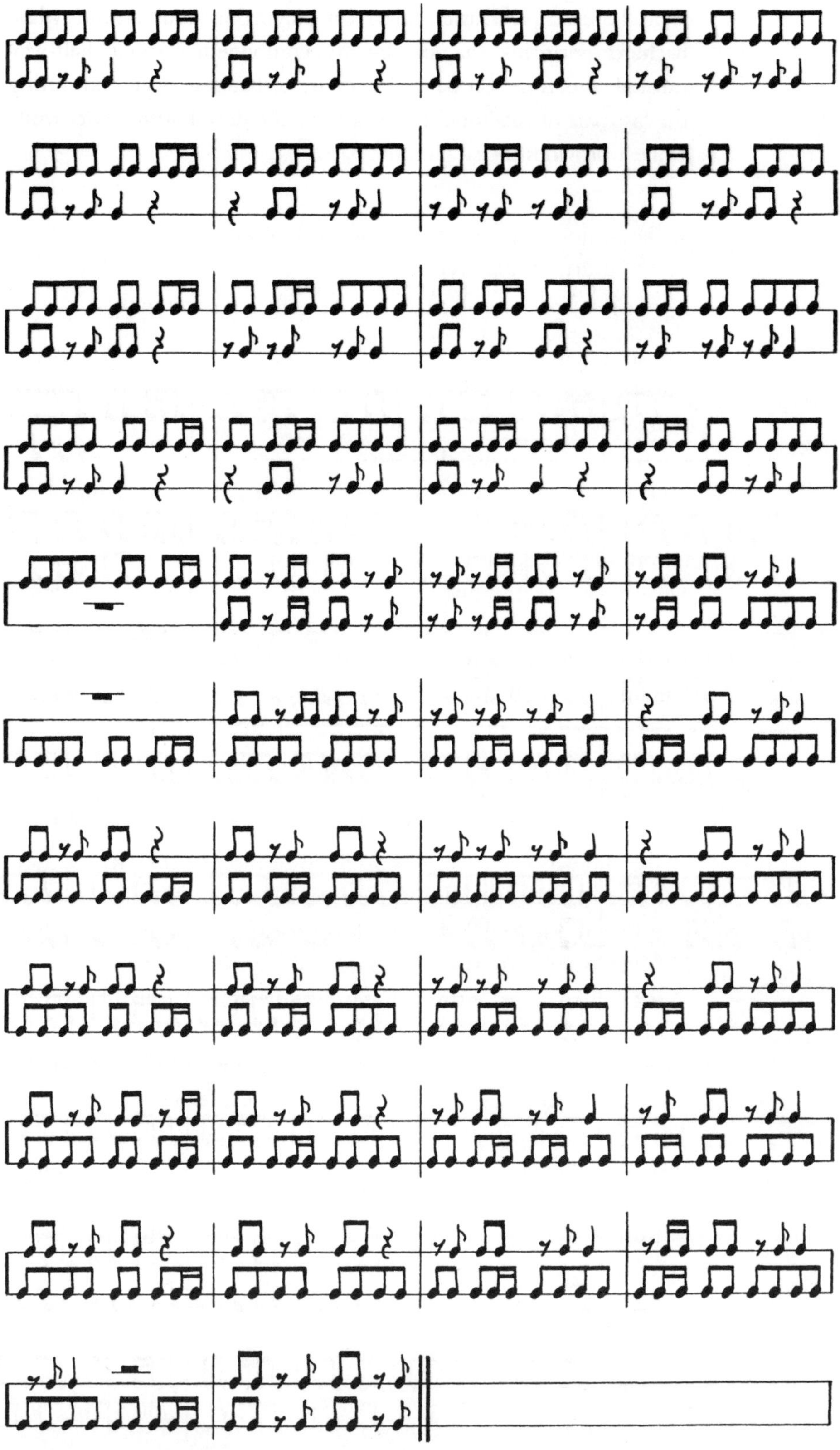

I have focused in this transcription on what the drums actually play. As the Lambeg is not damped in playing, it would also be possible to transcribe what the ear perceives. A rhythmic pattern such as ♫ ⁷ ♪♫ ⁷ ♪⁷ ♪♫ ⁷ ♪♩ (as used in the previous transcription) would then occur as ♫♩ ♫♫♩♫ ♫♫♩ .

The essential ornament in the double-time part is the roll, which occurs in this example in the form of ♫♫ . It is used frequently in the piece for ornamentation, but its double occurrance (a double meaning implicated in the term 'double-time') is not so frequent. Where it occurs, it usually occurs in bars 3 and 7 (except twice), but it is not essential that it always *has* to occur in these bars. It is rather that the accumulation of this ornamentation in specific places defines the regional styles, but there is a certain amount of flexibility left to the individual drummer.

There are also a few exponents of a 'triple-time' playing style; notably Kyle Dowie and Darren Sterritt. Within the drumming community, the mnemonic aid description of the roll would be by the word 'diddly', and a triple-time rhythm would be represented by lilting rhymes such as: 'Diddly diddly diddly dat de-dat, diddly diddly diddly dat de-dat de-dat'.

Fionnuala Scullion (1981:29) describes that the fifers almost always played selections of hornpipes from the repertoire common to many Irish traditional musicians, and that other tune types – such as reels or jigs – were 'dropped down' into hornpipe time. That is, 4/4 and 6/8 became 2/4 time, and the reels and jigs were slowed down to the more manageable speed of the hornpipe. She gives a transcription of a Lambeg-and-fife tune, which she recorded in Dromara, Co. Down, in July 1980. It shows clearly how the single-time Lambeg drumming style syncopates the melody played by the fife.

As far as the double-time drumming style is concerned, Fionnuala Scullion describes that there exist two distinct forms, referred to by their practitioners as 'breaking' after 'three and seven', or 'breaking' after 'four and eight' (Scullion 1981:30). The different systems of 'breaking' are associated with the different drumming associations, and therefore with different regions. According to Fionnuala Scullion's description – and confirmed during my own field research – drummers recognise different areas associated with these drumming styles, and she describes relationships between different territories as characterised by slightly grudging mutual respect (Scullion 1981:30).

Fife time and accompanying single-time
Lambeg drum rhythm.

Played by three drummers in unison, Dromara, Co. Down, July 1980.

$\downarrow = 98$

Transcription: Fionnuala Scullion

FIG. 3.10

FIG. 3.11:
Instrument maker
Richard Sterritt playing
the 'Challenge Cock',
one of a pair of drums
made from the same
piece of timber.

During my own research I was told that the different drumming
associations came into existence because there were occasional fights
between drummers from the different territories over decisions at
drumming matches. The split into different drumming associations
is reported to have widely resolved these problems of regional rival-
ry, although this is, of course, no guarantee for fair decisions at
drumming competitions. Fionnuala Scullion dates the formation of
the first drumming associations to 1950, and by now there are five
drumming associations in existence: Ulster, Mid-Ulster, Lagan
Valley, Antrim, and Armagh and Down. But the split into different

drumming associations does not just serve to eliminate rivalries. It also supports different regional musical interests, and there is a certain overlap of membership between them. Richard Sterritt for instance, is a member of all these associations.

In the photograph Richard Sterritt demonstrates how the sticks are held in playing the Lambeg drum. The instrument shown is the 'Challenge Cock', one of a pair of drums made from the same piece of oak. The twin drum is a 'plainshell', a drum without painted decoration. Richard Sterritt claims that the painting of drum shells has a negative effect on their sound qualities, and that this clearly shows in a comparison of these two twin drums.

The Bodhrán

The requirements for the preparation of the Bodhrán head before a musical performance are of a somewhat different nature to those of the Lambeg. But likewise, the attention is focused on achieving a particular tone quality. A standard instrument does not have any provisions for tightening or loosening the skin. Consequently it is the skin itself which receives treatment to prepare it for a suitable playing condition. In warm, dry weather the skin may need to be moistened; more often the skin is slightly slack because of prevailing Irish weather conditions, and it needs to be warmed up and dried out before playing can begin. Further treatment may be required after playing the instrument for a while, as the player's hands – and in particular the left hand – are in contact with the skin during performances, and they therefore exert an influence on the skin's humidity and temperature.

At present, there are various different techniques employed for playing the Bodhrán, but most frequently a double-ended wooden beater is used for this purpose. For the related playing technique the stick is held in one hand – normally the right hand – similar to a pen, and the bottom end is used for the accented beats – in an upward/downward alternation movement achieved by turning the wrist – while the top end of the stick is used for adding ornamentation; such as triplets.

The technique described above is regarded as a 'standard' technique, but individual musicians employ various different or additional methods for playing the instrument.

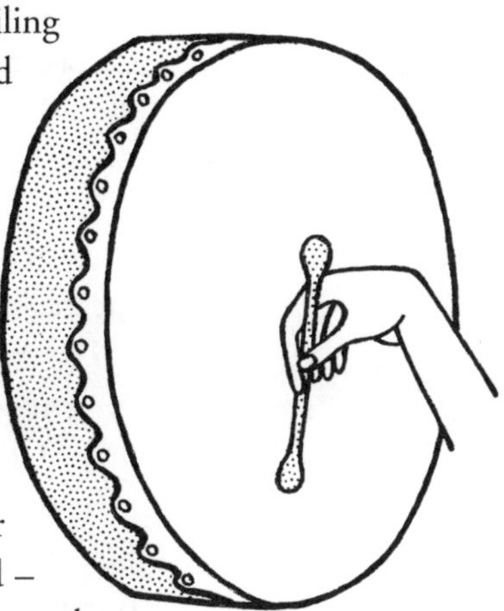

FIG. 3.12:
Hand position for playing the Bodhrán

Whichever style of playing is employed by the player's right hand, there is an additional aspect involved for varying the sound, and this is executed by the player's left hand. In performance, the left hand is placed inside the drum – against the skin – where it can slide up and down to vary the sound; for instance by damping it, or by altering the skin tension. Some players will only hold the Bodhrán by the cross-bar and play with their right hand; with or without stick. But most musicians will use a combination of movements of both hands in their performances.

A number of terms are used for the traditional wooden stick used in playing; such as 'tipper', or the Irish word 'cipín'. As the shape of the stick closely resembles the shape of a bone, it has been suggested that the instrument may originally have been played with a bone. This idea is not far-fetched, as rib-bones are also used to provide percussive accompaniment in traditional Irish music. Instrument maker Séamus O'Kane thinks that the Bodhrán was never played with a bone, and that the assumption arose from a mistranslation of the word 'cipín', which can also mean 'bone'. I have found no evidence of this, as various dictionary entries referred without exception to 'something woody', such as a little stick or a twig. Maybe it is not essential to answer this question, as evidence would be hard to come by. In any case it is not only the traditional cipín, which is used nowadays for playing the instrument. Present-day Bodhrán playing strives for variety in sounds, and while most players keep a selection of wooden sticks of varying length, weight, and size for this purpose, there are also some musicians who experiment with softer sounds, such as those produced by playing with a jazz brush.

The repertoire of music in which the Bodhrán is normally used consists to a large extent of traditional Irish dance melodies, and the role of the Bodhrán is seen as an accompaniment to the various melody instruments used in this musical genre. In playing, the Bodhrán closely follows these melody instruments, and its accentuation usually stresses the same notes as are emphasised in the melody. In principle it is the accented beats of the melodic line which are emphasised by the main strokes on the Bodhrán, although the player may choose not to play on *all* of these. Ornamental triplets on the Bodhrán are added in the same fashion as they are employed by melody instruments.

A typical performance of traditional Irish music with Bodhrán accompaniment may sound like this:

Example of Bodhrán playing

Melody Instruments

Bodhrán

Stick (Bottom) Movement

(the middle notes of the triplets are played with the top of the stick)

As in Lambeg playing styles, technique depends essentially on the combination of alternating movements, and in Bodhrán playing this balance arises from the combination of upward and downward strokes. There are a number of tutors available – such as Ó Súilleabháin 1984, or Hannigan 1991 – which explain in detail how these different strokes can be combined in playing. Although there are different playing styles in existence, they cannot easily be categorised, as variants are strongly coloured by the tastes of individual musicians. Mícheál Ó Súilleabháin uses the broad categorisation of playing with a two-knob stick – which he terms 'North Kerry' style – and playing with a one-knob stick – termed 'West Limerick' style. The latter style he sees as closely related to the hand style (Ó Súilleabháin 1974b). But in the same text he points out that neither style is confined to these districts, and the regional terminology could therefore lead to misunderstandings. Eric Cunningham, who is interested in contemporary performance practices, employs a categorisation into five playing styles: the 'two-ended stick style', the 'one-ended stick style', the 'brush style', the 'hand style', and the 'two-handed style'. But he modifies his categorisation by pointing out that he uses the model only for analytical purposes, that the terminology is uncommon among musicians, and that elements of any two or more of these styles may overlap in practice (Cunningham 1999:23).

In other words: there exist no clear-cut categories in Bodhrán playing, and in either case all styles have in common that they tend to follow closely the rhythmic structure of the melodic line. This does not mean that individual players do not consciously use means of

FIG. 3.13

syncopation. But if syncopation is employed, it is normally used as a variant to the traditional rhythmic structure of the music.

A fairly traditional structure is employed by The Chieftains in their recorded version of the 'Wren Song'. Wren songs have a long tradition in Ireland, and in performances their words were adapted to suit regional and individual circumstances. Their historical background is further discussed in Chapter 4.

♩ = 216   **The Wren Song** (Chieftains version)

FIG. 3.14:

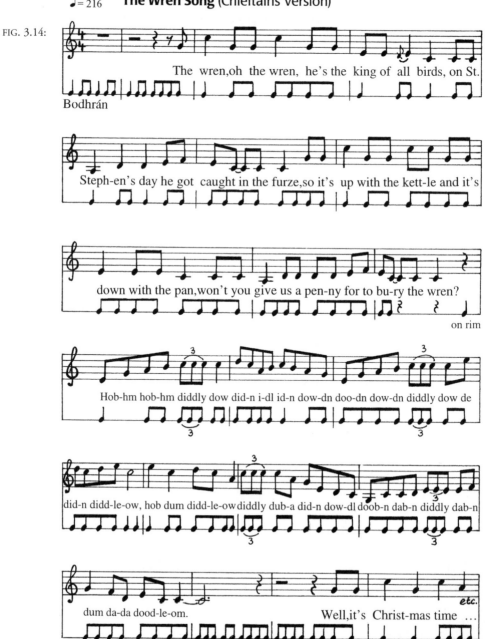

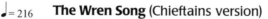

The Wren Song (Chieftains version)

The wren, oh the wren, he's the king of all birds,
On St Stephen's day he got caught in the furze,
So it's up with the kettle and it's down with the pan,
Won't you give us a penny for to bury the wren?
Chorus (lilted)

Well, it's Christmas time, that's why we're here,
Please be good enough to give us an ear
For we sing and we dance if youse give us a chance
And we won't be coming back for another whole year.
Chorus

We'll play Kerry polkas, they're real hot stuff,
We'll play The Mason's Apron and The Pinch of Snuff,
John Moroney's Jig and The Donegal Reel,
Music made to put a spring in your heel.
Chorus

If there's a drink in the house, would it make itself known
Before I'll sing a song called The Banks of the Laune;
A drink with glubrimication in it
For me poor dry throat, and I'll sing like a linnet.
Chorus

Oh please give us something for the little bird's wake,
A big lump of puddin' or some Christmas cake,
A fistful of goose and a hot cup of tae,
And then we'll all be going on our way.
Chorus

The wren, oh the wren, he's the king of all birds...

The first verse of the song is a traditionally transmitted component common to all Wren songs; and the additional verses were written in the traditional manner by Kevin Conneff. Kevin told me that John Moroney, a whistle player – also known as 'the farmer' – was a close friend of Willie Clancy. The text reference to 'a fistful of goose' also relates to an event involving John Moroney.

A considerably less conventional playing style is employed by Eamon Murray (see Fig. 2.6, page 52) who gives the following long introduction to a set of reels (The Maids of Mount Cisco/Ed Reavy's Reel) performed by the group Ceoltóiri Crosskeys:[5]

5 Broadcast on Downtown Radio in 2000, in Tommy Sands' programme 'Country Ceili'.

Improvised Bodhrán introduction

Performer: Eamon Murray

Bodhrán

Melody Instruments

FIG. 3.15   Eamon's performance displays a wide variety of tones and timbres of the Bodhrán. The frequent rhythm changes appear to have been employed in a casual manner, as they show no relation to the following piece(s) of music, and his main purpose seems to lie in a display of variety in playing the Bodhrán. The loose rhythmic structure reflects the freedom of style and high component of improvisation in the playing of the instrument. The high variety of timbres, on the other hand, also reflects the specialisation of the instrument maker – Séamus O'Kane – to provide Bodhráns with highly sensitive skins. Eamon Murray comes from Loughbeg, Co. Antrim.

Bodhrán introductions to traditional pieces of music are not employed normally in community music making, as they are not seen as a part of the traditional role of the instrument.

Gill from Belfast is a community musician (see Fig. 2.5 page 51). She uses session playing as a means of relaxation from stress at work. Gill describes her own playing style as highly idiosyncratic, but in fact she plays very much in the traditional manner, mostly with a double-ended stick, and closely following the melodic structure provided by the other instruments. She has tried Bodhrán classes at the Crescent Arts Centre in Belfast and thought that the teaching was very good, but she became afraid of being pushed into a 'standard' playing style; so she left the classes at an early stage. 'I just play what's in my heart. And what's in my head, and what my hands do, you know? And I'm sure the way I play would horrify a lot of Bodhrán players. But it's just what comes to me, and I enjoy it.' It seems that her heart and her hands beat very much in time with the musical tradition.

Gavin O'Connor from Belfast has taught the Bodhrán for over ten years; for most of this period in the Crescent Arts Centre. He says that from the very beginning there had been a great interest in his classes. Although he has now divided his classes into a 'beginners' and an 'intermediary' group, he still has problems with over-subscription to his classes. Gavin describes how he would teach his pupils a variety of basic rhythm patterns, but that from a very early stage he encourages his pupils 'to follow their own creative urges'. Improvisation is encouraged, and the result is that all participants – including Gavin – discover new elements in every class and thereby increase their personal repertoires. Gavin also encourages his pupils to experiment with sounds, for instance by playing with different sticks and brushes. Musical literacy plays no role in the classes, but Gavin uses tabulature transcriptions, for instance from Mícheál Ó Súilleabháin's (1984) Bodhrán tutor. He also uses tapes with traditional music – for his pupils to play along with in the

FIG. 3.16:
Bodhrán teacher Gavin O'Connor

classes, and to practice at home.

Another means he employs are little rhymes, similar to those used in teaching the Lambeg. One of them goes 'crash crash chronic weather, come let us dance together', while another one runs 'Ronald Reagan beats me – Maggie Thatcher, money snatcher, one two three'. Apparently these rhymes have not been passed on from a previous generation, but on the other hand they seem to have an element of already being 'history'. Maybe in the long run Gavin will only use little lilting rhymes like 'Boom ba dada' (for reels) and 'Boom ba dadada' (for jigs). But as Gavin says, everyday language provides a lot of three and four-syllable words, which can be drawn on at any time.

Learning about the Bodhrán certainly also has its light side. Gavin recounts a story of when he was telling his class about putting a bit of oil on the Bodhrán skin to make it more supple. Later on during the same class Gavin mentioned that a new Bodhrán skin can be quite scratchy, and that a method to soften it would be to fill some water into the turned-over drum and to swill it around for a minute or two before drying it off. Apparently one of his pupils had mixed up the two ideas in his memory, because, as Gavin describes it, 'suddenly, at the beginning of the next class, an overpowering smell like from a chippy filled the classroom.' As it turned out, the pupil had purchased a bottle of cooking oil and had poured it into the drum. Gavin says it took him indeed a very long time to dry out his drum, but it was certainly not scratchy anymore. Of course, care of the drum also has to be learned. Normally, instrument makers will provide some useful tips when asked for advice.

Comparison of the playing of the drums

From the above description of the playing styles of the two different drums it can be seen that each instrument requires a completely different handling in playing. Although rhythmic structure and ornamentation have a lot in common, the sound qualities produced on either of them are of a completely different timbre. Another difference shows in the body posture adopted in playing the drums. While the Lambeg is normally played in a standing position, the Bodhrán is most often played in a sitting position – except for its use in the Wren Boys/mummers tradition, which depends on body movement during performances.

With the Lambeg drum, an influencing factor for its playing

position is certainly the fact that the body of the drum plays an important part in its sound amplification. It is likely that, had the instrument been played in different contexts, its morphological features would have developed historically in a different way. As far as the Bodhrán is concerned, the player's body posture is rather insignificant in relation to its sound amplification, but it is important for its playing style. In fact, a lot of detailed ornamentation can only be achieved in a sitting position, as the left hand can slide more freely, since it does not have to carry the weight of the instrument, which is resting on the player's leg. But it is very likely that the reverse holds true as well: that the custom, common among musicians, of sitting down together for playing traditional music has influenced the playing style of the instrument.

Some ornamental figures – as, for instance, the use of triplets – are common for both drums and for different playing styles. Syncopations are another stylistic feature which occurs in the traditional musics of the Lambeg as well as those of the Bodhrán. But the Lambeg is better known for this feature, as some Lambeg playing styles are structured upon the use of syncopations; whereas in Bodhrán playing syncopations tend to occur rather as a variation of an otherwise rhythmically aligned percussive accompaniment to the performance of the melody instruments. When looking at the playing of the two drums in relation to traditional dance melodies, the emphasis of each drum could be described as being applied at different points within the musical structure. It could therefore be said that the two instruments fulfil complementary roles in relation to this musical genre.

Exploratory projects

Societies can be very strict in their views of what are acceptable playing styles. In his book *Different Drummers* Michael H. Kater describes how jazz rhythms in pre-Nazi Germany came to symbolise trends towards modernism and emancipation (Kater 1992:17), which were forcibly suppressed in later years when the Nazis came to power in Germany.

Currently in Ireland, the Bodhrán and the Lambeg have come to stand as symbols of two different traditions – sometimes termed the 'Catholic' and the 'Protestant' traditions. On a pragmatic level this categorisation shows in the fact that musical projects which make use of both drums, are seen within society as 'culturally exploratory and innovative in character'. By conservatively minded musicians and audiences they would be regarded as 'deviations from the tradition'. Some people even hold the opinion that the respective playing styles are so completely different that the two drums should in fact not be combined at all.

The performance transcribed below addresses the issue of cultural expectations about the role of the two instruments in present-day Northern Irish society. It was recorded in 1996 during two days of public debate at The Queen's University of Belfast, which was initiated by Rostrevor, Co. Down, singer/songwriter Tommy Sands.[6] The event included a variety of cross-cultural musical contributions and one of these came from the group 'Different Drums'. The two drums were played by Roy Arbuckle and Stephen Matier, and it is worth pointing out that both musicians are performers on both instruments – which is by no means common in contemporary Northern Irish society. On 'Listen to my Heartbeat' Roy Arbuckle plays the Lambeg and Stephen Matier the Bodhrán.

Listen to my Heartbeat

Live performance at Queen's University Belfast, 8-8-96

Roy Arbuckle: Lambeg
Stephen Matier: Bodhrán

FIG. 3.17

The musicians described to me that for them the underlying idea of 'Listen to my Heartbeat' was to 'get away from the militaristic association of the drum', and that their main inspiration came from the Japanese Kodo drummers. 'Listen to my Heartbeat' is based on one of their pieces, from which the part derives that is played here on the Lambeg. The Bodhrán part was added by the musicians themselves, and their introduction was inspired by North American Indian culture.

From an analytical point of view, it is interesting to note that despite the innovative character of the piece, both drums remain fairly close to their traditional role: the Lambeg part is fixed within the piece, while the Bodhrán part is flexible and shows a fair amount of variation and improvisation. The Bodhrán is, of course, a more flexible instrument. It is more suited for playing fast tiny details of ornamentation, as it makes use of a damped sound, while the Lambeg depends for its natural timbre on a ringing sound. The insertion of triplets occurs widely at random, which is also the case when the Bodhrán is played in its traditional context. But the Bodhrán player also integrates syncopated figures which are normally associated with Lambeg drumming styles, and they are used here to achieve a call-and-response effect. The Lambeg does not make use of any of its traditional ornamental patterns: neither triplets nor syncopations occur in the piece, nor do any rolls.

The instruments play in close relation to each other, and the effect of 'speeding up' is achieved by an increasing density of increasingly shorter note values. The Lambeg pattern develops from playing one crotchet per bar to playing two crotchets per bar, then to four crotchets per bar, and then eight quavers per bar. In a parallel relationship the Bodhrán pattern develops from using crotchets to using quavers, and then to semiquavers, while making an increasing use of triplets. The process of accumulative density occurs four times in the piece.

From a stylistic point of view, it can be observed that both instruments combine traditional and innovative elements. Both drums rely on their traditional timbral qualities for their sound production, and both drummers make use of playing styles which divert from the traditional musical roles of their respective instruments. It is worth noting, though, that neither style digresses from the cultural expectations of a regular metre, which is associated with the western musical tradition generally. The stylistic components in this performance can therefore be said to derive their cross-cultural meaning from the culture-specific context of Northern Irish society.

Ideas of a broader cross-cultural nature can be found, for instance, in the music of Mícheál Ó Súilleabháin and Mel Mercier. Eric Cunningham describes Mel Mercier's Bodhrán playing as making use of 'non-Irish musical ideas, such as Indian polyrhythmic structures' (Vallely 1999:32). An example would be their piece '(must be more) crispy', different versions of which can be found on the albums 'Gaiseadh/Flowing' and 'Between Worlds'.

A stylistically exploratory project is also Neil Johnston's 'Wrap it up', with a musical arrangement by Arty McGlynn. This is a swinging rap rendition, integrating traditional Irish tunes, and dealing with the role of a Bodhrán player in a traditional band. It can be found on the album 'Shifting Gravel' by the group 'Four Men & A Dog', with Gino Lupari on vocals. This is a flavour of its lyrics:

> Listen, you people, better take this down:
> I'm the Bodhrán player, and I'm back in town
> It's me lays down the rhythm for Diddery-y-de-dee;
> There ain't no Flashy Fiddlers any good without me.
> I can do it on the Bodhrán, I can do it on the Bones,
> I don't need no fancy drum kit like the Rolling Stones...
> You can keep your fiddle player, your banjo pickin' man,
> But the man who minds the goatskin is the leader of the band.

4
The historical and mythological background of the two drums

My drumming pattern was Aunt Kauer's black silken, multiply buttoned dress. Confidently I can say that I succeeded in dressing and undressing the wrinkled and skinny spinster several times a day on my drum, by unbuttoning her and buttoning her up again with my drumming, but not necessarily having her body in mind.

The Tin Drum, Günter Grass, 1960:58

Drums are found in numerous cultures worldwide, and they are among the instruments most often associated with symbolic meanings. In a number of cultures drums are said to 'speak with the voices of the ancestors', and in some African cultures drums are decorated with carvings representing these ancestors. In African contexts drums may also symbolise royalty, and such drums will only be handled and played by select people.

In Brazilian *candomblé* drums are regarded as sacred instruments, and they will only be played by initiated musicians. Shortly after construction of the instruments a sacrilisation ceremony is performed, during which the drums are sprinkled with a sacred liquid. Sometimes ceremonial food and drink offerings are made to the drums. In *candomblé* rituals the drums are used as a means to communicate with the gods, but they are also seen as having a 'voice of their own', which is said to be 'irresistible to the gods' (Béhague 1984:229–37). *Candomblé* is a possession cult, which has its roots in African (Yoruba) religion.

Shamanism also uses drums – notably frame drums – as a vehicle to make contact with the spirit world. The Buriat people, who live on the shores of Lake Baikal, tell a creation myth about their shamanistic drum, in which their first shaman, Morgon-Kara, retrieves a human soul from the high lord of heaven (Cotterell 1986:97–8). Shamanism is found in many cultures worldwide, although with the introduction of the major world religions, shamanistic rituals were often driven underground. Many survived in the form of storytelling or as folk customs. Even particular playing styles associated with these rituals were often transmitted over many centuries.

Over the last few centuries, Ireland has been influenced essentially by European concepts about music, mainly through the common European art music tradition. European cultures have in common that they associate drums with military meanings, and it is indeed the military who have developed and preserved the fife-and-drum tradition in Europe.

But it is not just history in which we will find explanations for symbolic meanings of our drums. As in other societies, different layers of meaning will be found in myths and folk tales associated with the instruments. From an anthropological perspective it it therefore not desirable to draw a clear dividing line between recorded history, oral history, and mythology. Meanings overlap, ascribed myths reflect society's values, and additionally all symbols carry ambiguous meanings (cf. Douglas 1966). All these meanings may be relevant at any time, although their interpretations may shift, depending on the context. This chapter looks at various facets of meanings ascribed to the Lambeg and the Bodhrán within present-day society.

The Lambeg

As far as the Lambeg drum is concerned, its mention in recorded history dates back at least to the nineteenth century. Fionnuala Scullion relates that the historical Belfast instrument maker William Hewitt claimed the first Lambeg drum to have been made by his grandfather in 1870. This drum is reported to have been constructed from a single piece of oak – as opposed to staves, with which some earlier drums were made (Scullion 1981:20). Likewise, Portglenone instrument maker Jack Wilkinson claims that drum making has been in his family for three generations, and this also takes the craft back well into the nineteenth century.

Older history intermingles with myths, many of which relate to the end of the eighteenth century, i.e. the period of the French Revolution. In Irish history this period coincides with the battle of the Diamond (1795) and the time of the formation of the Orange Order – which makes it an appropriate period to be associated with the Lambeg drum. Neil Jarman (1999:25–6) quotes a historical source of the period, which refers to 'drum and fife' as having been used in a 1796 parade.[1] The 'drum' is not specifically described in this source, but it is likely to have been a military type of drum – an ancestor of the modern Lambeg.[2]

There are also various myths and folk tales in circulation, which tell of these drums having been brought over from the European continent around the time of the battle of the Boyne (1690) by King William's men. This may well have been the case, as a drum of similarly large dimensions shows in Rembrandt's 1649 painting 'The Night Watch' (Scullion 1981:20). One drummer gave me his personal version of how the drum developed in Ireland:

> You see, it used to be on the side of the horse. You know, the way they had the drums on the side of the horses. Kettle drums you call them. That's what they started on, as they came across them in the sixteen-hundreds. But you know, the Irish being very thick, say, 'What a horse can carry we can carry' [laughter] So they put a strap round the neck and hung it round the neck. They didn't have horses, you see? So they say, 'Oh, we can take that there, we're horses, we're a horse of men.' So that's how they started. That's how it came to be hung around the neck.

Although this account may not be accurate, it can be seen that older-time myths relate to a military connection of the drum. The instrument's morphological features do in fact confirm this suggestion, as they closely resemble those military drums that were played in combination with the fife in eighteenth century Europe.

Janet McCrickard describes the 'French connection' and a 'military theme' as also being found in a number of myths connected with the Wren tradition, details of which are discussed later in the Bodhrán

---

[1] A description of an early parade taken from a letter from Lord Gosford of Markethill to Lord Camden, the lord lieutenant, in Dublin, dated 13 July 1796.

[2] Fionnuala Scullion (1981:20) gives a description of an early drum marked with the name of Walsh the drum maker and dated 1849. The instrument resembles present-day Lambeg drums, but it is slightly narrower and considerably smaller in diameter (18 to 23cm smaller) than today's average-size drum.

FIG. 4.1:

The 'Wren Drum', made by Richard Sterritt, and decorated by Eamon Maguire. One side (above) depicts the legend of the wren warning soldiers about an enemy by pecking on their drum.

FIG. 4.2:

The other side (below) depicts the legend of the wren becoming the king of all birds by outwitting the eagle.

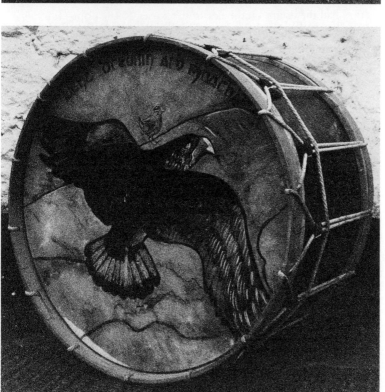

section: '… the drum is the bodhrán itself, or an unspecified drum, or one of the 'fife-and-drum variety' (McCrickard 1987:27).

A number of folk tales are told about the wren, various military settings, and the theme of betrayal. In these the wren is said to have warned particular armies by hopping or pecking on a drum. The armies are either those of King William or of Oliver Cromwell (Killen 1986:133), the Danes or the English (McCrickard 1987:27), the Vikings (Danaher 1966:30), or the Norsemen (Danaher 1959:667). One version of the tale, told about the Siege of Derry, refers specifically to Lambeg drums.

The drum as a symbol of military associations occurs also in folk songs; for instance in the traditional anti-war song 'Arthur McBride':

> And the little wee drummer
>   we flattened his pow [head]
> And we made a football
>   of his row-de-dow-dow [drum]
> Threw it in the tide
>   for to rock and to roll
> And bade it a tedious returning.

Large-size drums in other cultures often have religious meanings attached to them – like, for instance the Japanese *Taiko* drums; or drums in North American Indian cultures, which would be played by a group of people sitting around them. Of similar dimensions to the Lambeg drum is the *Surdo* used in Brazilian carnival music. It is damped in playing, and the body posture adopted in performance is that of a side drum. The *Zabumba*, a drum used in popular Catholicism performances of the Brazilian *bandas de pífanos*, is made in different sizes. The largest drums look remarkably like smaller-size variants of Lambeg drums: they are supplied with ropes and buffs for tuning, and they are approximately the size of the present bass drum in Ireland. They are also played in an upright position, but while their right head is played with a padded stick, their left head is played with the hand or with a tiny wooden stick. This gives the drum a considerably softer sound than the Lambeg. And – also at variance with the Lambeg – to accommodate the weight of larger drums, the musicians may sit down for their performances. The *Zabumba* drums are played in combination with small, side-blown bamboo flutes, somewhat reminiscent of fifes. Some musical components of the genre are likely to have been brought to Brazil by

European (Portuguese) settlers (cf. Allgayer-Kaufmann 1996). Most larger-size drums in other cultures are either played with the hands or with padded or unpadded wooden beaters, and many of them are damped in playing. This makes it likely that a reciprocal influence has taken place in the development of the Lambeg drum between its morphological features, its playing styles, and its use within specific cultural contexts.

Over history, different sizes and different materials have been experimented on for making Lambeg drums. This applies to their heads as well as to their bodies (Scullion 1981:22). For instance, a number of shells have been made from brass. They gave good stability, but they turned out too heavy for carrying the drum.

Instrumental in the change of the sound of the Lambeg drum and its playings styles was certainly the changeover to cane playing sticks, which is said to have taken place in the late nineteenth century. Historical evidence can be found, for instance, in a photograph of the Drumbeg Purple Star LOL 638, dated 4 April 1893, in which canes can be seen for use in playing the Lambeg drum[3] (see Fig. 4.4 on page 90).

Previous to this changeover, the ancestor of the present Lambeg drum was played with a pair of wooden sticks. Fionnuala Scullion describes that instrument maker William Hewitt ascribed the origin of the name of the drum not to the often mentioned first use of the drum at the historical meeting of 1871 at Lambeg, but to the first use of the canes (Scullion 1981:36, 1981:21). One of the results of the changeover to canes has been a considerable increase in volume of the drum. Fionnuala Scullion describes an experiment of a sound pressure level measurement

FIG. 4.3:

This brass shell from Moira, Co. Down is painted inside (plain) and outside; the wooden centre and mouth hoops are attached to the shell with rivets.

Photograph by Bobby Magreechan.

[3] The photograph was part of a travelling exhibition entitled 'Symbols' (1994), promoted by the Community Relations Council, and put together by curator Rhonda Paisley in cooperation with Tony Buckley.

FIG. 4.4:

Drumbeg Purple Star
LOL 638, dated 1893.
This photograph was
taken at the back of
their lodge room at
Bob Stewart's public
house. The fifer can be
seen in the back row
wearing a cap. He was
employed for the day
and paid 30/-.

during the playing of a single drum, which showed results of around 120 decibels (Scullion 1981:36, 1982:73). This level is generally regarded as the threshold of pain for the human ear. Fionnuala Scullion refers to the Ulster author Lynn Doyle as mentioning that in the late nineteenth century the playing of such powerful drums – in particular when provided with ass skin heads – was said to have been forbidden by law, because of their window shattering might (Scullion 1981:21).

Religious symbolism abounds in relation to the decoration of the Lambeg drum, and it also shows in descriptions of the instrument. The sound of the drum is being associated with that of a bell; a religious symbol in many cultural contexts. Roly Sterritt describes the sound of the drum as likening 'the sound of a church bell on a lovely Sunday morning, when you lie in your bed, and you hear the bell ringing in a distance, calling you to worship'. The symbol of the bell is also used by the Sterritts on their drum heads, to indicate their makers. The associated sound of a bell is also sometimes reflected in names of drums, such as 'The Chiming Bells of Laurelvale', 'Humming Bells of Craigs', or 'The Bells of Ballylisnahuncheon' (Scullion 1982:36).

Motifs used in the decoration of the Lambeg drum also use religious symbolism and reflect biblical themes, but their symbolic meanings are multilayered, expressing different themes at the same time. For instance, an old, early twentieth-century, William Johnson instrument I was shown depicts 'Samson and the Lion', on the surface a biblical theme (Judges 14). But the biblical theme also includes the imagery of the beehive (Samson finds a bees nest and honey inside the rib cage of the lion). And the bell and the beehive imagery is also used to describe a drummer's psychological condition in drumming competitions, where the competing rhythms are said to explode in the drummer's head into the sound of a beehive and a bell.

FIG. 4.5:

Piece of Sterritt skin, showing the symbol of the bell

Other mystical ascriptions to the playing of the drum are that in performance the stick is supposed to 'hit you in the ear', and you should 'feel electric in your hair'. This condition is said to 'move stones on the ground in the vicinity'. A drum with such sound qualities would be described as 'having a hive of bees in her', which is a symbolic description for a supreme instrument. One drummer said that a drum like this would sound 'like a whole choir, with the alto and the soprano, and the men on the bass, and it brings all the range of tones together'.

When adding to this description the terminology for playing the drum, which was explained in the previous chapter, an extremely interesting pattern emerges concerning concepts about music within the drumming community. Drumming patterns are termed 'tunes', and speech rhymes are termed 'songs'. And a drum 'sings with many different voices'. Drummers hear fine differences in tone, for which the western art music tradition has no separate categories. Clearly, the drumming community has *its own musical categories*. These have to be held in mind for discussing this music, as an assumption of congruence with western art music terminology will lead to great misunderstandings.

Apart from the individual use of themes of decoration for individual drums, each Lambeg is said to have its individual sound, and each instrument has its individual mythical story attached to it.

Fintan Vallely (1995) tells that the 'Ballylane Cock' is 'a thief'; that it 'steals' the tone from other drums in competitions. Carol McCracken tells of a drum known as 'The Smasher'; a name derived from an unusually high number of broken heads ascribed to the drum (McCracken 1996:51).

'The Mystery', made by William Hewitt, is said to have arrived under mysterious circumstances, and it has a reputation of liking to disappear and reappear. Richard Sterritt tells a story of how the drum acquired its name and its reputation:

> Well, in our country there's a wee drum called 'The Mystery'. And how she came about was, there was three gentlemen bought the drum between them. And they were quite wealthy men, and they didn't mind forking out the money at the time for the drum. And they thought they would take her out and try and compete against men in the same Lodge as them. And it worked out that they hadn't the knowledge nor they hadn't the capability, and they couldn't get the drum up nor down nor in or about, nor they couldn't work her at all. So they hadn't told anyone else, and they'd only had her at home in their own houses, trying to get the drum right to take her out. And they decided that it was a mission, that they won't ever gonna get her right. So they decided that they would take the drum down in the wintertime, when all the old drums were put back into Teemore Hall. And they'd put the drum in, and they'd say nothing about it. So this is what they'd done. When the boys came back, when the regular drumming men came back to lift their drums out at the start of the season again, to compete again, they walked into the Hall, opened the door, walked in, and they seeing all their drums sitting, and lo-and-behold, they seeing this three-foot plainshell drum, and a note on top of her saying 'The Mystery'. So this name stuck with her, because nobody knew where she came from, or anything about her. And the man that owned her, or claimed her, from Teemore, was a wee man called Jimmy McFadden. He's dead and gone, but his nephew Raymond McFadden told me all about it. His son Kyle McFadden now owns her. And it transpired that the three men concerned, one of them let slip, and that's how they found out where she came from.

And this is how the drum became 'The Mystery'. So there we have an origin myth of a drum from within our own cultural context. (In a variant of this myth the drum is said to have arrived on a train from Belfast, without any note from the sender.)

In descriptions of the Lambeg anthropomorphisms are used within the drumming community; e.g. the drum has to 'breathe', and 'she' has to be strong. The status of the drum as a 'female' drum shows also in the use of skins of she-goats only in its construction, and its female role is sometimes alluded to in the use of sexual imagery in folk poetry. Also the drum has 'mouth' hoops and 'flesh' hoops, and over time a whole body of myth builds up around each individual instrument, which gives the drum 'her' personality. It can be inferred from these descriptions that for people involved with the drum there exists no such thing as 'a Lambeg drum'. There exists a traditional craft to costruct the drum, but once the instrument is made it is 'imbued with life of its own', and it will from then on be referred to by its individual name.

Lambeg drums were also used by the Ancient Order of Hibernians (AOH), a nationalist/Catholic institution. There are various folk tales in circulation about members of the AOH and members of the Orange Order negotiating – or even fighting – over the possession of drums which had a reputation of having particularly good sound qualities. There are also tales told about loan exchanges of drums having taken place between both organisations, as their marches would have taken place on different days. In the case of painted drums temporary decorations were used to dress the drums according to the occasion.

Compared to the Orange Order, the Ancient Order of Hibernians had very few drums, and the Owen Roe O'Neill drum is one of the very few surviving Hibernian drums in Ireland. For Hibernian drums please refer also to colour plates 4 and 5 on page xvii.

Brendan MacAnallen from the Brantry area, Co. Tyrone, told me the story of this drum as it was told to him by Joseph McGeough (deceased) of Ballycastle, Brantry, Dungannon, Co. Tyrone. The AOH was established in the Brantry area during the mid nineteenth century. Joe's family were members of the AOH, and Joe described the AOH as descended from the society known as 'Defenders'. The AOH died out in the Brantry area in the mid twentieth century, but as the AOH Hall was adjacent to Joe's house, all their memorabilia (drums, banners, etc.) survived. The Owen Roe O'Neill drum is one of a pair of drums – the other one being the Robert Emmet drum, which is in the process of being repaired – and both drums had a reputation for excellent sound qualities.

Joe related a story about a group of people from the Brantry area, led by Harry Hamill, who carried the two drums from Ardboe

FIG. 4.6:

The 'Owen Roe O'Neill' drum is one of a pair of Hibernian drums from the Brantry area, Co. Tyrone. It is around a hundred years old, and it was made from a single piece of oak.

Central to Legane, a townland adjacent to Carrycastle, in the early 1890s. Joe reported that there was a ban on drums around this time (cf. also F. Scullion's reference on page 90), and that the drums had to be carried during the night to Legane. Owen Roe O'Neill is associated in Irish history with the Ulster Rebellion of the seventeenth century, and in particular with the battles of Curlew Pass and of Benburb, both of which took place in the 1640s. The drum was repaired and touched up by instrument maker James Hamilton of Carrickfergus, Co. Antrim, (see Fig. 1.16 on page 12) and it can be seen occasionally in exhibitions.

The Bodhrán

As far as recorded history is concerned, it is extremely difficult to trace the origins of the Bodhrán in Ireland. Previous to its rise in popularity as a result of the 1960s folk revival, mention of it is found in folklore studies of farming contexts rather than in descriptions of music-making. The most comprehensive text available on the Bodhrán is Janet McCrickard's lovingly designed folklore study,[4] which traces the instrument back to its use as a skin tray. Skin trays were used in farming contexts in Ireland and in neighbouring countries; mainly for chaff separation, but also for baking, keeping and serving food, or as a storage container for various household implements (McCrickard 1987:1–16).

Similar frame drums are found worldwide, and various theories have been suggested as to how the Bodhrán may have come to Ireland. Instrument maker Eamon Maguire's suggestion is that the drum may have come from the Middle East with the first farmers who settled in Ireland. While this may well be the case, it is just as likely that similar frame drums were invented independently in different cultural contexts. Either theory makes it impossible to trace the historical origins of the drum, as it may have arrived within the farming context at practically any point in history.

The oldest historical reference to the use of the Bodhrán as a musical instrument comes from Kevin Danaher, who describes a tradition of its use in combination with the old Irish bagpipes to produce martial music 'in the days of the Earls of Desmond' (Danaher 1959:669). This is a rather flexible time indication, but it dates the use of the instrument in Ireland back at least to the early seventeenth century. But the Bodhrán may indeed have been in use in Ireland for a considerably longer time, as it is historically associated with its use by the Wren Boys. It has been suggested by various authors (Danaher 1958:558, 1966:30, Such 1985:12, Muller 1996–7:151) that the Wren ritual may have its roots in pre-historic, or at least pre-Christian, times. Other authors think it more likely to have originated from the medieval morality plays (de Fuireastail 1973:3), while McCrickard (1987:30) suggests that the Wren ritual may well derive from a mixture of these influences, and that the Bodhrán may have been added to the Wren tradition through introduced elements from the 'folk-play', which has its roots in pre-Christian spring rites.

When taking Kevin Danaher's description of the early musical use of the Bodhrán into consideration, it could well be that the skin tray had been in use in Ireland – and put into annual musical use by the

[4] *The Bodhrán* (1987) is designed in calligraphy and illustrated with hand drawings by Janet McCrickard.

Wren Boys – and that a particular playing style (for instance the double-ended stick style) was imported from France around the early seventeenth century for performances of a particular musical genre. Janet McCrickard reports that her research showed only one other frame drum worldwide to have been played with a double-ended stick – the now obsolete French *mailloche double* – and being variously known as *tampon/tampion/tompion*. She suggests that this may hint at a French connection of playing styles (McCrickard 1987:28–9).

As far as written history is concerned, there are a number of texts which describe the skin trays for farming and household use, and the drums for use of the Wren Boys on their annual processions, to have been made in the early twentieth century in the home (Killen 1986:132, McCrickard 1987:1–6). These instruments were sometimes made by children in an improvised way, but there was also a fine craft in existence. Traditional methods were to use a bent willow branch (Evans 1957:279), semi-fossilized bog wood, or thick straw rope, around which the skin was lapped (O Súilleabháin 1974a:4–5, Such 1985:11, McCrickard 1987:5).

Janet McCrickard (1987:1) distinguishes two types of 'wechts': the shallow one for winnowing grain, and the deep one used for household storage purposes. Apparently both types were put into use as drums by the Wren Boys, although the winnowing wecht would have had a pierced skin, which would have directed it from its tone and volume into the category of 'emergency use'. Nevertheless both shapes can be used to produce a frame drum – i.e. an instrument with an unpierced skin.

It is likely that the present shape of the Bodhrán – with its deep frame – was influenced by agricultural mechanisation processes in the early twentieth century, which provided ready-made frames of household sieves and riddles that were no longer needed. These could be used for the construction of Bodhráns, and some instrument makers also inserted jingles into their rims. (On traditional sieves and strainers see Danaher 1962:35.)

Various playing styles are reported in relation to the Wren tradition. The most common ones seem to have been the 'hand-style' and the 'double-ended stick style', but Kevin Danaher mentions also the technique of playing 'with one short drumstick' and that of 'two sticks held in the same hand' to be used by the Wren Boys for playing the Bodhrán (Danaher 1966:28–9). Bodhrán playing styles seem to have varied considerably; as they do indeed today as well. But one thing that is certain is that the 'double-ended stick style' is not an invention of the 1960s folk revival and Seán Ó Riada's popularisation of the instrument. The stick technique – and other playing styles – can be observed in various of Kevin Danaher's historical photographs taken in the region of Co. Limerick (cf. Danaher 1955, 1966).

FIG. 4.7:
Bodhrán player, Athea, Co. Limerick, dated 1946.

Photograph: Kevin Danaher.

An interrelationship between the Wren Boys' performances and other mumming and rhyming traditions can be observed, not only in a partial overlap of repertoire, but also in the costumes employed. The Armagh Rhymers told me that the items used in dressing up always have a background history in the community; so they will express symbolic meanings to the people involved. One of the characters in the folk play is dressed up in an old style military uniform, and often so is the 'captain' of the Wren Boys (cf. Fig. 4.8 on page 98). Other common paraphernalia are straw costumes and masks (cf. de Fuireastail 1973:2–3, Muller 1996–7:142), and occasionally animal horns (Evans 1957:279), which are said to have derived from a pre-Christian tradition associated with spring rites (McCrickard 1987:13, 30).

There are certainly deeper layers of meaning from various centuries hidden in the Wren ritual. Sylvie Muller suggests that the wren may represent man, and that man's changing relationship with nature from the Neolithic period onwards may be reflected in different types of wren tales (Muller 1996–7:146–51). There is also a sacred theme attached. The wren was considered a holy bird by the ancient Druids, and James Frazer describes many European peoples – the ancient Greeks and Romans, the modern Italians, Spaniards, French, Germans, Dutch, Danes, Swedes, English, and Welsh as designating the wren as the 'king', the 'little king', the 'king of birds', or the 'hedge king' (Frazer 1922:536). Sylvie Muller adds to this list the Russians and the Polish (Muller 1996–7:131).

The ritual associated with the Wren Boys is reported as common

FIG. 4.8:
Wren Boys with
costumes,
Co. Limerick, 1946.
Photograph: Kevin
Danaher.

in Ireland, England, Scotland, Wales, the Isle of Man, and France,[5] although in Scotland and Ulster it seems to have been known only in a few places (Danaher 1959:672). In most places the money collected at the Wren Boys' parade would be used for a Wren party held on some evening shortly afterwards, which was accompanied by music and dance (Danaher:1959:672). In Ireland the wren is tabooed except on Christmas Day and St Stephen's Day, when it was hunted for its ascribed 'treacherous character'. One version of the wren tale tells of the bird betraying St Stephen hiding from his prosecutors in a gorse bush. There are many variants of the story in existence.

In many parts of Ireland the wren was hunted and killed, and displayed in a holly or ivy bush, by the Wren Boys on their musical house-visiting tour on St Stephen's Day. But the Armagh Rhymers told me that in Ulster it was considered unlucky to kill the bird. So the wren was displayed in a *wren box* – a decorated little cage –

[5] Kevin Danaher (1959:672) describes how in France the wren was ceremonially hunted with huge clubs, guns, and swords, which would be more suitable for hunting larger animals.

on St Stephen's Day, and afterwards it was released (cf. Muller 1996–7:144). In the contemporary Wren Boy tradition symbolic effigies of a bird are displayed during Wren Day visits.

All recorded versions of the 'Wren Song' are disjunct, and their meaning is not at all clear. The Armagh Rhymers kindly gave me their version of the song. Theirs is a jig version (compare also the reel version of The Chieftains in Chapter 3), which they combine with different instrumental tunes to go with the song on different occasions. The jig that is combined here with the song is called 'The Lilting Banshee'.

The Wren Song (Armagh Rhymers version)

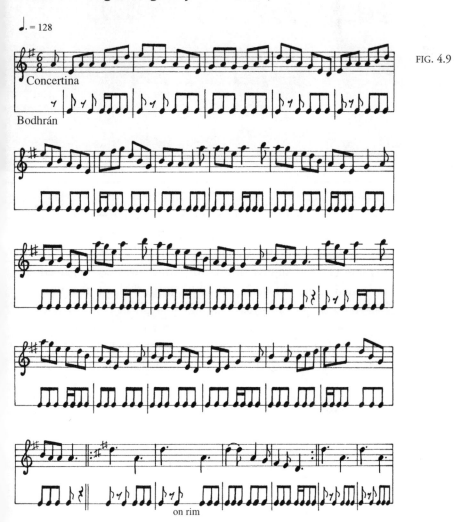

FIG. 4.9

Oh, Mister ...'s a worthy man, and to his house we
A   bunch of ribbons by his side, the Armagh boys to

brought the wren, ramb-ling round as you can see, it hangs u-pon a
be   his guide, al-though he's small, his family's great, up and give your

hol-ly   tree.
neighbours a treat. Hur – rah, me boys, hur – rah.

Oh Mr... is a worthy man
And to his house we brought the wren;
Rambling round, as you can see,
it hangs upon a holly tree.
A bunch of ribbons by his side,
The Armagh Boys to be his guide.
Although he is small his family is great,
Up and give your neighbours a treat.
Hurrah, me boys, hurrah!

Dreoilín, dreoilín, where's your nest?
It's in the woods that I love best,
Under the holly and ivy tree,
and the Armagh Boys come hunting me.
The wren, the wren, the king of all birds,
On Christmas day was caught in the furze.
We hunted him up and we hunted him down
And in the woods we knocked him down.
Hurrah, me boys, hurrah!

On Christmas day I turned the spit,
I burned my finger, I feel it yet,
Between my finger and my thumb
Came a blister as big as a plum.
I have a small box under me arm,
A few pence more will do no harm.
If you fill it of the best
I hope to heaven your soul will rest.
If you fill it of the small
It won't agree with the Wren Boys at all;
Up with the kettle and down with the pan,
Give us your answer and let us be gone.
Hurrah, me boys, hurrah!

As far as decoration is concerned, nowadays the frames of Bodhráns are usually plainly decorated, i.e. they are treated with stain (wood dye), French polish, and varnish. The skins may be left plain, or they may be decorated with ornaments. If skin decoration is used, its themes are often derived from Celtic mythology and/or its related ornaments. Christian themes appearing in the decoration will usually derive from the Book of Kells, which itself drew on pre-Christian art and symbols.

FIG. 4.10:

Instruments of the
Armagh Rhymers,
made and decorated
with individual
traditional themes by
Eamon Maguire.

The instruments of the Armagh Rhymers are made by Belfast
Bodhrán maker Eamon Maguire, who carries out all his decorations
individually by hand. The drum on the right represents a famous
theme from Irish mythology, which is told about Queen Meabh and
the Cattle Raid of Cooley (Táin bó Cuailnge). The drum on the left
depicts the mummers themselves. The drum at the bottom was made
by Eamon from an original old household riddle, by removing the
wire and replacing it with skin. The poem on the drum refers to the
rhymers as music makers, and its underlying idea is that poetry and
music (ceol) is the same. The text of the poem reads:

And as the twilight
Flithered on the heather
Water music filled the air
And when the nighttime
Came down upon the bogland
With all-enveloping wings
The coal-black turf stacks
Rose against the darkness
Like the tombs of nameless kings.

Comparison of the historical and mythological associations of the drums

When looking at the historical and mythological background of the Lambeg and the Bodhrán, it becomes obvious that both instruments carry culture-specific meanings, which cannot be inferred solely from their morphological features. The cultural symbolism of the instruments must therefore have resulted from a combination of aspects. Among these will be found their historical associations as well as symbolic meanings for which their decoration has come to stand within their cultural context.

It is worth noting that both drums are decorated with paintings, and that neither makes use of any carvings, although some instrument makers are also wood carvers. This suggests a connection between the development of the two instruments, as carving is a technique of decoration applied to many drums worldwide.

A point which seems to me of particular importance in relation to symbolism assigned to drums within western cultural contexts – and this applies to the Lambeg as well as to the Bodhrán – is their association with war, signalling, and with military contexts. This type of symbolism emerges often in tales told about the two instruments. A part of this symbolism may have derived from the fact that the percussive element is relatively under-developed within western musical cultures and that the status ascriptions to percussion sections within the western art music tradition are found at the lower end of the spectrum. The combination of all these cultural meanings predisposes drums to stand for military symbolism. As a consequence their role is seen by society as that of a rhythmic accompaniment at a regular metre secondary to other instruments. These meanings are culturally constructed within society, and they are ascribed to the instruments from the outside rather than by the musicians themselves.

Musicians, on the other hand, tend to perceive primarily the musical role of the instrument they are playing, and this shows in the playing styles of the Lambeg as well as the Bodhrán: in the hands of a skilled musician the resulting sounds can be vibrant, multifaceted, and most interestingly structured.

5
Images of the drums within society

In the County Tyrone near the town of Dungannon
There was many a ruction meself had a hand in.
Bob Williams he lived there, a weaver by trade
And all of us thought him a stout Orange blade.
On the twelfth of July as it yearly did come
Bob played on his flute to the sound of a drum.
You can talk of your harp, your piano, or lute,
But nothing compares to the old Orange flute.

from 'The Old Orange Flute', trad.

In many cultures worldwide symbolic meanings are ascribed to musical instruments. Ireland is no exception. In present-day Irish society the Lambeg and the Bodhrán have come to stand as symbols of 'Protestant' and 'Catholic' culture. This is a rather crude classification system. In the previous chapters we have seen that neither drum is exclusive to either cultural grouping. Both are – and have been – used in various different contexts. Historically, the Lambeg has a background in Catholic culture as well as in Protestant culture. And as far as the Bodhrán is concerned, it is highly unlikely that all farmers in previous times, who used farming riddles etc., were Catholics.

In his essay 'Thoughts on Celtic Music' Malcolm Chapman talks about the construction of musical categories of 'self' and 'other', and he notes that the contents of such categories can change continuously, while the categories themselves remain (Chapman 1994:36).

Also, the distinction between 'self' and 'other' is relative, as it depends on the wider cultural context. Michael Herzfeld cites an excellent example of two neighbouring Cretan villages, the inhabitants of which are at daggers with each other over an old feud, but who would use expressions of a common regional identity within the city context of Athens (Herzfeld 1987:217–8).

The previous chapter has shown that historically neither the Lambeg nor the Bodhrán have a solely 'Protestant' nor a solely 'Catholic' background. Neither do the musicians fit neatly into these emblematic categories. Most musicians see themselves primarily as musicians, and many of them do not construct their identities around religious or political categories. In this chapter I will look at how these constructed images of the drums affect musicians in performances, and how the images are used in turn by the musicians – and other artists – to express their own views on these topics and on ascribed roles within contemporary society.

The Lambeg and the Bodhrán
Image constructions and their use within society

One of the least discussed topics in relation to the Lambeg and the Bodhrán is gender. In the previous chapters I have pointed out that there is a male ethos surrounding the Lambeg drum. The drum itself is considered a 'female' drum, and aspects of virility are associated with its playing technique. I talked to Caroline Stewart from Armagh, and I asked her whether she was the only female Lambeg drummer:

> At the minute, yes. Although you do hear that there's one or two girls who used to play years ago. But they didn't actually play in competitions. They just played at the house. I think I was the first one to play in an actual competition, so I am the only girl.

Caroline started playing the Lambeg about five years ago, and around three years ago she started to enter competitions. Since then Caroline has won a number of first, second, and third prizes, and she has even judged at one competion, which people described as 'very well judged'. I asked Caroline about reactions from the 'male world' of Lambeg drummers. Were they surprised? Were they supportive? Or were they confused by her presence? 'I think the majority of them are surprised. But they were supportive, yes. And there's one or two of them, who are not so keen on you. And they will tell you.' It seems that the 'male world' of Lambeg drummers is in the process of adjusting to a female competitor.

Caroline describes further how many of the drummers do not easily accept any comments from her about *their* drumming, but that they are all good company when the competitions are over. In other words, we find the 'classic' situation of a gendered society, which tends to question the competence of a woman more than that of a man. But then, of course, Caroline is also quite young in comparison to most Lambeg drummers. Caroline takes it all with a shrug. She thinks that times are changing, and in the meantime she likes to focus her attention on improving her drumming techniques, as she genuinely enjoys playing the drum.

A slightly different situation arises in relation to the Bodhrán. Eric Cunningham describes the Bodhrán as 'a male-ethos instrument in the past' (Vallely 1999:32), but there is scant evidence for this – except maybe for a short period in the 1960s (when all publicly visible musicians seem to have been male).[1] Ireland is a gendered society, and the musical activities of women have indeed been left out of the historical records for a long time (cf. Bowers and Tick 1986, MacCurtain and O'Dowd 1991, Schiller 1999). But if the Bodhrán was originally a skin tray used in farming contexts, which is said to have been employed occasionally to provide percussion to house dances (Such 1985:12),[2] there is no reason to assume that women – who did their fair share in the winnowing and other farmwork – should not have participated in contributing musically to house dances. In fact the skin tray is one of the most likely instruments they would have chosen to contribute to these (historically unrecorded) merriments.

Be that as it may, Gill, a Belfast community musician, describes being confronted with image constructions relating to the Bodhrán. Her experience does not relate to gender ascriptions of the instrument, but to the other image construction attached to the drums, i.e. the Catholic/Protestant image. Gill comes from a Protestant background, and she has members of the Orange and Black institutions

[1] In the 1960s Seán Ó Riada was highly influential in popularising traditional Irish music – including the use of the Bodhrán – nationally and internationally. In his 1960s radio series (published as Ó Riada 1983) he propagated a concept of this musical genre as a 'vigorous masculine music'. Consequently, publicly well-known traditional Irish music groups of the period did not include any female musicians, although the old folk tradition of playing this music in the home was carried on by musicians of either gender.
[2] Such refers to an eye witness account given by the Co. Sligo traditional musician Séamus Tansey, which relates to the 1950s.

in her family tree. She loves playing drums, and she started playing the Bodhrán a few years ago with some traditional Irish musicians at sessions. She does not see any political associations in drums whatsoever. She is captured by the different rhythms, and she describes an experience she had a few years ago at a St Patrick's Day session in Morrison's Bar, Belfast. She had come in after work, to join a group of musicians, who had been playing already for a few hours.

> A group of three fellows were standing close by, shouting out tunes first to play. And then they came over at one stage and [one of them] said, 'Can I have a go on your drum?' And at that stage I was exhausted, and I said, 'Yeah, go ahead.' So he picked it up, and asked me how to hold the stick, and how to hold the drum. And I showed him, and he tried to have a go, and he just couldn't get his rhythm right. And he turned round to me and said, 'You see, it must just be in youse. You have something, you are born with that', assuming that I was Catholic, therefore Celtic, therefore able to play the Bodhrán drum. And I just smiled and I said, 'Is that right?' He says, 'Definitely, definitely. You see, we haven't got that. Youse have got something we haven't got. Not much, but that's it, it's in you, you're born with it.' And he gave me back the drum, and he said, 'Where did you start playing anyway?' And I said, 'Well, actually Carryduff Accordion Band.' And he looked at me and he said, 'Carryduff?' And I said, 'Yeah, the Accordion Band.' And he said, 'Ah, alright love. Cheerio then.' Because he obviously assumed that if I played in a Celtic band, or in a traditional band, that I must be from a different persuasion than himself. And when I said that I started playing the drum in the Carryduff Accordion Band – which he knew, was a Protestant Twelfth band – he was somewhat confused.

Gill thinks that society has 'moved on a bit in the last couple of decades', and she describes how she enjoyed causing 'a bit of confusion to those old mentalities that are still there'.

In her study of historical processes of image constructions, Doris Dohmen explains that historically constructed images have a tendency to persist independently of immediate experiences of social reality (Dohmen 1994:10). In relation to the two drums this would mean that particular images have become attached to them, and that these images linger on, irrespective of changes within society.

Belfast musician and Bodhrán teacher Gavin O'Connor gave me an assessment of the distribution of pupils in his classes over the last ten years. He describes the Catholic/Protestant balance among his pupils as approximately equal – 'besides people from various other persuasions, like shamans, Sikhs, and Buddhists'. The gender distribution he sees as 'traditionally more in favour of females', and the age distribution in his classes ranges 'from 6 to 70+ years'.

This does not mean, of course, that present-day Irish society does not consciously use these ascribed images of the drums for symbolic expressions. The contentious issue of Orange parades through nationalist areas – much discussed in the press in recent years – is the topic of a cartoon by Belfast artist Cormac. His cartoons have been a part of Belfast's counter-culture for about three decades, and they have long reached world fame. Cormac is associated with the nationalist side of northern Irish society, but quite often he expresses a third point of view, which does not easily fit into any categorisation. His cartoons often speak for various disadvantaged groups in society. This cartoon looks at the issue of loyalist marches from an outsider's perspective. Of course, the Bowler Hat and the Lambeg Drum are used as the 'classic' symbols of Orange culture.

Anthony John Clarke is a singer/songwriter from Holywood, a town on the outskirts of Belfast, who now lives in Liverpool,

FIG. 5.1:

Cormac cartoon, July 1996

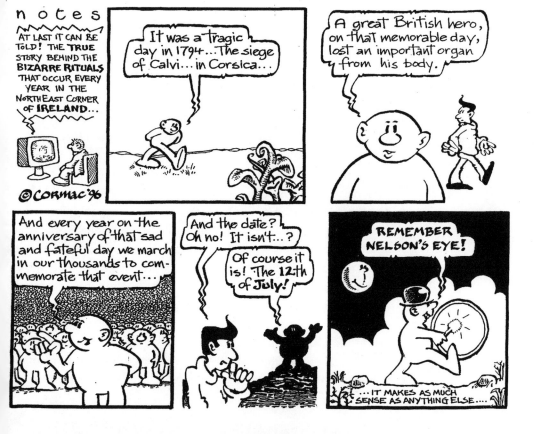

England. Anthony John also comes from a Catholic/nationalist background, but he takes a completely different perspective on Orange parades. This is how Anthony John describes the song in his introductory notes on the cover of the album:

> When I was a small boy I used to watch the parades in July from my bedroom window in Holywood, Co. Down. I really envied the boys in the street who got five shillings for holding the colourful banners. As it says in 'The Broken Years' [another fine song from the same album] most of us just want to walk down the same street.

Marching   Anthony John Clarke

♩ = 192

FIG. 5.2

It's the March-ing Sea-son,   there's gon-na be a big pa – rade,

it's the March-ing Sea-son,   tell the child-ren to bring lem–on – ade;

mud on the road from the rain last night, so   take your old cloth–es, be

sure to take a litt-le mon-ey with you this year,the shops they are not

closed. I   guess these   years must count for   some-thing,   for

some-thing do they not? For I used to stay in – doors 'bolts and

locks'.   Take the lad–der from my win – dow and stack your bon–fire

high,   let the bog – ie man climb back in – side his box.

It's the Marching Season,
There's gonna be a big parade,
It's the Marching Season,
Tell the children to bring lemonade.
Mud on the road from the rain last night,
So take your old clothes,
Be sure to take a little money with you this year,
The shops they are not closed.

Chorus:
I guess these years must count for something,
For something do they not?
For I used to stay indoors 'bolts and locks'.
Take the ladder from my window
And stack your bonfire high,
Let the bogie man climb back inside his box.

It's the Marching Season,
I'm your neighbour! 'How d'ya do?'
It's the Marching Season,
Let me fly your flag for you!
Babies tangled in the bunting,
A pretty girl in a hat,
Father Michael and the vicar sharing snickers,
Where did they get that?

Chorus

It's the Marching Season,
There are deckchairs on the street,
It's the Marching Season,
Oh the pipe-smoke's smelling sweet.
Every bar on every corner,
Every house in town,
The volume's up on all the music
And the barricades are down.

It's the Marching Season,
Why don't you leave your car at home?
It's the Marching Season,
A marquee with lots of microphones,
The Telegraph is taking photographs,
Big Gerry's gonna have a laugh,
The parish priest is giving autographs
And we'll all be on the news.

Chorus

It's the Marching Season,
I'm gonna launch my big campaign,
It's the Marching Season,
I'll give it a fancy nancy name,
We can all wear uniforms
And we can all hold hands,
The boys can be in dancing teams
And the girls can be in bands.

Oh it's the Marching Season,
Time for some champagne!
The Marching Season,
This year's route's been rearranged,
There's crowds about, all the schools are out,
There's a Ministry of Fun,
Tap your feet to the steel band
Or bang the Lambeg drum.

Chorus

Musically – and textwise – an off-beat song, Anthony John focuses on the positive side of parades by using their carnevalesque image. As usual, Anthony John looks at events from his own angle, which does not easily fit into ready-made categories. This song comes from his latest CD 'Man With a Red Guitar'.

Yet another view on the topic emerges in Mickey McConnell's song 'The Lambeg Drummer'. Mickey comes originally from Ballinaleck, Co. Fermanagh, and he lives now in Listowel, Co. Kerry. His song uses the image of the Lambeg drummer to express effects of the politico-cultural divide in present-day Northern Ireland by means of telling an individual love story. Over the years, Mickey has been adding and changing words of the song. This particular version comes from a live performance in the winter of 1995–96. The song has been released recently on an album entitled 'Joined-Up Writing'.

The Lambeg Drummer

♩ = 128

Mickey McConnell

I met her on a far Greek isle, our ac-cents I-rish, I glanced a smile.

This girl I could not love at home, I loved in Greece, and lat – er Rome,

on through France and the dust of Spain, Christ, I'll nev-er love like

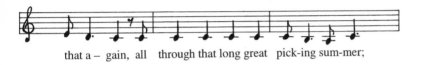

that a – gain, all through that long great pick-ing sum-mer;

now she's the wife   of a Lam-beg Drum-mer.

FIG. 5.3

The Lambeg Drummer

I met her on a far Greek isle,
Our accents Irish, I glanced a smile,
This girl I could not love at home
I loved in Greece and later Rome,
On through France and the dust of Spain
Christ, I'll never love like that again,
All through that long great picking summer;
now she's the wife of a Lambeg drummer.

And she touched my cheek in Brittany
'What a shame you're Mick, not Sam', said she,
'Or Stewart, Cecil, Ian, Rob,
Or Billy, Ivan, Jack, or Bob,
For you're locked inside some Celtic/Fenian dream,
You long for things that might have been,
But let's not waste what's left of summer
Before I wed my Lambeg drummer.'

We wandered a deserted beach;
Though I held her hand she was out of reach,
Side by side, but both alone
As we thought about the news from home.
And I knew it was time for letting go
Of this sweet and most beloved foe
For her ears were tuned for tribal thunder
That called her home to her Lambeg drummer.

And in a drab Dutch town we said goodbye;
I had to hitch, she had/chose to fly.
T'was only when she turned to go
That I told her what she had to know
That, had she been Mary, Briege, or Kate,
We'd have walked together out the airport gate
And I'd never more be parted from her
By time or tide or a Lambeg drummer.

And I watched the Orange Twelfth parade,
I was half impressed and half dismayed;
There I saw the girl I loved
All hatted, sashed, bemedaled, gloved,
More lovely than she'd ever been

When she was Orange and I was Green
And her love outblazed the Spanish summer
That's squandered now on a Lambeg drummer.
And had she been Mary, Briege, or Kate,
We'd have walked together out the airport gate
And I'd never more be parted from her
By time or tide or a Lambeg drummer.

Having looked at how the Lambeg drum appears in artistic images when seen from outside its own cultural context, this is how the Lambeg drum may appear when seen from within its own cultural context by a Lambeg drummer himself. This poem was kindly given to me by the Sterritt family from Markethill. It was written by Roly Sterrit about the construction of his brother Richard Sterritt's Lambeg drum.

In the summer of '87 Dick Sterritt brought home some oak.
It was 12 foot long, over 1 foot wide, and its purpose was bespoke.
A plank of coffin oak it was, for burying in the ground,
But Dick had another thought for it: to create a beautiful sound.
It was American red oak, grown through wind rain and sun;
When cut and planed and turned, it would make a Lambeg drum.
To Frankie Orr's of Lambeg was where bold Dick he went;
He there explained his projects, and worked till the cash he spent.
Frank worked all through the winter with Victor at his side
To make a drum for all to hear, and carry Dick's name with pride.
In the summer Frank said, 'She's ready, I'll give oul' Dick the phone.'
Dick sent his brother Roly, saying 'Go and bring her home.'
Dick kept her in his bedroom to get her fully dried;
He looked upon her lovingly, impatient to have her tried.
At Donaghmore she was unveiled and rang out like a gong;
Says Herbie Power, 'Dick knows a plank, for she can sing a song.'
With Kyle Dowie on the sticks he was rolling off the swell;
You'll hear her ring for miles away: big Dick's playing as hell.

But to return to the Bodhrán: the drum is not just used occasionally as a nationalist symbol; it also comes in for a fair bit of satire from within the community. Irish society is predominantly conservative, and if the western art music tradition sees its percussion section as lower-status instruments, then a percussive instrument within the native folk tradition is likely to be classed within the same status range. This is how the Belfast broadcaster Tony McAuley describes it:

'Some musicians can't stand the sight or the sound of them [Bodhráns], and there is an old joke doing the rounds, which suggests that the best way to play a Bodhrán is with a razor blade.'[3]

There are in fact a few of these 'Bodhrán-jokes' in circulation, and they all make fun of the Bodhrán's claim to status as a musical instrument. One of them asks what is the difference between a Bodhrán and an onion, and its punchline is that people cry when you cut up an onion. Another one tells of a man getting on a train with a strange case under his arm. When asked about it by his fellow passengers, he declares it to be a machine-gun (bomb, bag of semtex). To which a passenger replies, 'Thank goodness, I thought it was a Bodhrán.' Yet another asks what you call a fellow who hangs out a lot with musicians; to which the answer is: a Bodhrán player.

I am sure there are more of these in circulation, but the general vein of them will have become obvious by the above examples. It is the role of the drum as a musical instrument, that is used to elicit laughter from the listener who, of course, is assumed to know that drums are only used for 'banging on them' (see Chapter 2).

A considerably deeper layer of humour shows in a song written by Tim Lyons, which I learnt from the excellent singing of Cork singer/songwriter Tim Dennehy,[4] who now lives in Co. Clare. This song gives the good advice that, if you want to buy a Bodhrán (even if you happen to come from Germany), your best choice would be to get it from one of the qualified Bodhrán makers. The song has recently also been released on the album 'Big Guns and Hairy Drums' by the duo Scithereedee (Tim Lyons and Fintan Vallely).

Heindrich's Doolin Disaster (The Bodhrán Song)

Words: Tim Lyons
Trad. arr. Lyons/Dennehy

♩. = 108

FIG. 5.4

Oh, my name is Hein-drich Schnit-zel and from Ger-ma-ny I do come, of

all the mu-sic in the world I much do like the drum. I've late-ly been to

---

[3] Part 3 of the series 'Instruments of Ireland', see note 1, Chapter 1, page 15.

[4] Included on the CD 'Farewell to Miltown Malbay' (1997), see discography p130 for details.

Ire-land where mu – si-cia-ners play till dawn. 'Twas there my heart did

fall in love with a drum they call bodh – rán.

Oh my name is Heindrich Schnitzel
And from Germany I do come,
Of all the music in the world
I much do like the drum.
I've lately been to Ireland
Where musicianers play till dawn.
'Twas there my heart did fall in love
With a drum they call bodhrán.

One day I'm going to Doolin
Famed in music, song and dance,
And as I did hug my Fürstenberg
my mind was in a trance,
For there behind two fiddles,
In between a box and flute,
A thunderous bang and a goaty whang
The air it did pollute.

Oh this hairy drum my mind did numb,
In love with it I fell,
And I strongly did desire it
Despite the awful smell.
Enquiries then I soon did make
My mind being sorely bent
On if and when and where and how
I'd procure this instrument.

I approached this bodhrán driver now
Being drunken with the sound,
'To purchase one of these bodhráns

Will cost you fifty pounds.'
My blood did race at a gross pace
Beneath my wallet thick,
He then did roar, 'sixteen pounds more
For canvas bag and stick'.

'Oh mein Gott' then I'm exclaiming,
'This is most expensive loot.
At home we are not paying this
For a silvery concert flute'.
'Tisn't rightly known', says he to me,
'Nor I don't give a hoot,
So loan a gun from off someone
And your own goat you can shoot'.

Well this seemed to me a bright idea
And became my sole intent,
For we German Huns are good with guns
And brainy to invent.
That very day without delay
A shotgun I did borrow.
Says I, 'I'll have my goatskin now
This evening or tomorrow'.

Upon the Burren mountain-tops
I stealthily did creep,
Across its craggy rooftops
Into its valleys deep.
There suddenly appeared to me
A herd of mighty goats
With horns high and yellow eye,
Thick manes and shaggy coats.

As they thundered by I then let fly
my Ely's Number Five.
When the smoke had cleared it soon appeared
These goats were still alive.
I pursued them with alacrity
Till my legs were nearly lame.
It was no good, in vain I stood,
Back to Doolin then I came.

As I came up by Fisher Street,
My spirits dragging low
I heard a thick and heavy voice
Calling out, 'Hello, hello!
I observe a deadly weapon here
And pray is it your own?
Where is the licence for this gun?
To me it must be shown'.

'Well the truth to you I'll plainly tell,
No licence have I got
For I borrowed it from Jerry Smith
To have a sporting shot'.
'Jerr Smith how do, I'm arresting you
A subversive you must be
From some revolting movement
In far-off Germany'.

So here I lie in Ennis jail
Lamenting my condition.
The Gardaí found me guilty,
Ten pounds fine and extradition.
The sergeant swore me life away,
The judge he called me barmy,
'You're a Baader Meinhoff refugee
Or a member of Red Army!'

Farewell to Ireland's hills of green
far famed in song and poem,
Farewell to Burren's rocky slopes
Where wild Bodhráns do roam.
If ever I return again
I'll shoot no goat nor kid,
And when I want to play my drum
I'll pay up my fifty quid.

The Bodhrán can also be found in contemporary Irish literature, most notably in John B. Keane's novel *The Bodhrán Makers* (1986). The setting of his story is historically slightly ambiguous, and a theme that runs through the book is a criticism of clerical interference in secular affairs in Ireland in the past. Keane interweaves different meanings associated with the Bodhrán – old and new – to link

120

the past with the present, and he tells a story in which the instrument occurs in the central plot to express multilayered symbolic meanings and cultural values in Ireland. Ambiguity is a means used in many art forms, and in Keane's novel it is achieved through his use of the role of the Bodhrán.

Another novel about Irish drums is Seoseamh Mac Grianna's *An Druma Mór* (1969). Its story is based on historical events, which took place during the early decades of the twentieth century in the Donegal Gaeltacht,[5] and the contested instrument is a Lambeg drum, an druma mór. The drum belonged to a group who called themselves 'The Sons of St Patrick', and Mac Grianna's novel tells a humorous story about struggles having taken place over the

[5] A small Irish-speaking area in Co. Donegal.

possession of the drum between 'The Sons of St Patrick' and the Ancient Order of Hibernians (AOH). After political changes in the area, and the dissolution of both groups, the drum was kept in the Donegal Gaeltacht as an item associated with local history, but unfortunately it has since been destroyed by a fire.

Artistic ambiguity of meaning is also frequently employed in cinematography. An example would be the humourous short film *Skin Tight*, which was shown over the period around the Twelfth of July in 1995 on BBC 1 Northern Ireland.[6] The story of the film evolves around a Lambeg drummer who needs new heads for his drum, and his wife's pet goat. After family disputes, and the murder of the goat, its skin ends up being made into a Bodhrán.

The Goat

Having introduced a broad spectrum of people involved in the story-making – and history-making – of the Lambeg and the Bodhrán, I will leave the end of this book to the central character, who makes it all possible: the goat.

Goats have a history of early domestication in many cultures of the world, but there are also different species of wild goats in existence. Goats are fairly easy to keep, as they will feed on practically anything. They will live on plants that other domestic animals will not eat, and they can even eat many poisonous plants with impunity. They have even been reported to eat items of no nutritional value whatsoever – out of sheer curiosity.

Not surprisingly, religious symbolism has been ascribed to the goat in many cultures. James Frazer (1922:464–5) describes associations between corn-spirits and the goat, but also between tree-deities or wood-spirits and the goat, to be found widely in the folklore of northern Europe. He gives the example of the Greek deity Dionysos – a tree god – as sometimes being represented in goat-form, and of various other goat deities, such as the Pans, Satyrs, and Silenuses. Of course, Christian symbolism derived its image of the devil from the Greek god Pan. Traces of these ancient religious associations of the goat are nowadays found in folk tales all over Europe, and Ireland is no exception. An ancient custom surfaces, for instance, in the

[6] The film was part of the Northern Light series of three short films, a film co-production scheme between BBC Northern Ireland and the Northern Ireland Film Council. The film was written and directed by John Forte and produced by David Kelly for First City Features.

FIG. 5.6:
Children busking at
the Puck Fair (2000)
in Killorglin,
Co. Kerry

annual celebrations at the Puck Fair in Killorglin, Co. Kerry, during
which a maiden is symbolically married to a goat.

Present-day Irish society may not necessarily see any associations
with these ancient religious symbolisms, and the Puck Fair is indeed
a joyous event for young and old – with craft stalls, household wares,
toys and children's roundabouts. The fair also includes a fair amount
of music, and the Bodhrán is certainly found among the instruments

used in these performances. Nevertheless the goat remains with us in folk tales and mythology, and its mysterious symbolism shows, for instance, in the fact that particularly good sounds of drums – and in particular of the Lambeg – are sometimes described as deriving from certain character traits of the goats from whom the skins came (cf. Scullion 1981:33–4, 1982:203).

It seems therefore appropriate to leave the last word to the goat, and it comes in the form of another song I first heard from the fine singing of Tim Dennehy. It is included on his CD 'A Winter's Tear', but it has also been released on the cassette album 'When I grow Up' by the songwriter himself: Brian O'Rourke, from Co. Galway. Brian's interpretation is indeed a very fine version, which also uses a traditional musical style for its presentation. Brian told me that both, his song and Tim Lyons' Bodhrán song, were inspired by an event in the 1980s in Ullapool, Scotland, when the songwriters were looking at a postcard depicting the process of sheep shearing.

This is Brian's song, as it grew out of this inspiration. The goat has aspirations to become famous, and is looking forward to reincarnation in a future life as a Bodhrán.

The Bodhrán Song (When I Grow Up)

Words: Brian O'Rourke
Trad. Arr. Dennehy/O'Rourke

♩ = 208

FIG. 5.7

Oh, I am a year old kid, I'm worth scarce-ly fif-teen quid, I'm the

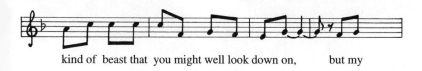

kind of beast that you might well look down on,   but my

val-ue will in - crease at the time of my de - cease,   for when

I grow up I   want to be a   bodh-rán.

The Bodhrán Song

Oh I am a year old kid, I'm worth scarcely fifteen quid.
I'm the kind of beast that you might well look down on,
But my value will increase at the time of my decease
For when I grow up I want to be a Bodhrán.

If you kill me for my meat you won't find me very sweet.
Your palate, I'm afraid, I'll soon turn sour on.
Ah but if you do me in for the sake of my thick skin
You'll find I make a tasty little Bodhrán.

Now my parents Bill and Nan, they do not approve my plan
To become a yoke for every yob to pound on.
Ah but I would sooner scamper with a bang than with a whimper
And achieve reincarnation as a Bodhrán.

I look forward to the day when I leave off eating hay,
And become a drum to entertain a crowd on.
And I'll make my presence felt with each well-delivered belt
As a fully-qualified and licenced Bodhrán.

And 'tis when I'm killed and cured, my career will be assured
I'll be a skin you'll see no scum or scour on,
But with studs around me rim I'll be sound in wind and limb
And I'll make a dandy, handy little Bodhrán.

Oh my heart with joy expands when I dream of far-off lands
And consider all the streets that I will sound on,
And I pity my poor ma who has never seen a Fleadh
Or indulged in foreign travel as a Bodhrán.

For a hornpipe or a reel a dead donkey has no feel
Or a horse or cow or sheep that has its shroud on,
And you can't join in a jig if you're a former Grade A pig
But you can wallop out the lot if you're a Bodhrán.

So if e'er you're feeling low, to a session you should go
And bring me there to exercise an hour on.
You can strike a mighty thump on me belly, back or rump,
But I thank you if you'd wait till I'm a Bodhrán.

[7] Idiom, meaning: the husband.

When I dedicate my hide I'll enhance the family pride,
And tradition is a thing I won't fall down on
For I'll bear a few young bucks who'll inherit my good looks
And be proud to know their auld one is a Bodhrán.

And I don't think I'll much mind when I've left himself behind[7]
Or regret I can no longer turn the power on,
For with a Celtic ink design tattooed on my behind
I can be a very sexy little Bodhrán.

Now I think you've had enough of this rubbishy old guff,
So I'll put a sudden end to my wee amhrán[8]
And quite soon my bloody bleat will become a steady beat
When I start my new existence as a Bodhrán.

[8] Irish for 'song'.

Bibliography

ALLGAYER-KAUFMANN, REGINE (1996), *Der Kampf des Hundes mit dem Jaguar: bandas de pifanos in Nordostbrasilien*, Eisenach: Verlag der Musikalienhandlung Karl Dieter Wagner.

BÉHAGUE, GERARD (1984), "Patterns of *Candomblé* Music Performance: An Afro-Brazilian Religious Setting", in *Performance Practice: Ethnomusicological Perspectives,* pp 222–54, ed. G. Béhague, London: Greenwood Press.

BLACKING, JOHN (1976), *How Musical is Man?,* London: Faber

BOWERS, JANE and JUDITH TICK eds (1986), *Women Making Music: The Western Art Tradition 1150–1950,* London: Macmillan

BRYAN, DOMINIC (2000), *Orange Parades: the Politics of Ritual Tradition and Control,* London: Pluto Press.

BUCKLEY, ANTHONY and MARY CATHERINE KENNEY (1995), *Negotiating Identity: Rhetoric, Metaphor, and Social Drama in Northern Ireland,* Washington and London: Smithsonian Institution Press.

BUCKLEY, ANTHONY ed. (1998), *Symbols in Northern Ireland,* Belfast: Institute of Irish Studies, Queen's University Belfast.

CARSON, CIARAN (1986), *Irish Traditional Music* (pamphlet), Belfast: Appletree Press.

CECIL, ROSANNE (1993), "The Marching Season in Northern Ireland: An Expression of Politico-Religious Identity", in *Inside European Identities: Ethnography in Western Europe,* pp 146–66, ed. Sharon MacDonald, Oxford: Berg.

CHAPMAN, MALCOLM (1994), "Thoughts on Celtic Music", in *Ethnicity, Identity and Music: The Musical Construction of Place,* pp 29–44, ed. Martin Stokes, Oxford: Berg.

COTTERELL, ARTHUR (1986) (first ed. 1979), *A Dictionary of World Mythology,* Oxford: Oxford University Press.

CUNNINGHAM, ERIC (1999), 'John Joe Kelly': Sticking with the Roots, unpublished MA thesis, Cork: University College Cork.

DANAHER, KEVIN (1955), (Ó Danacháir, Caoimhín), "The Bodhrán – A Percussion Instrument", pp 128–30, in *Cork Historical and Archaeological Journal*, vol. 60, July–Dec. 1955.

DANAHER, KEVIN (1958), "Happy Christmas", pp 556–60, in *Biatas – The Beet Grower*, Vol.XII (9), Dec. 1958.

DANAHER, KEVIN (1959), "Hunting the Wren", pp 667–72, in *Biatas*, Vol.XIII (9), Dec. 1959.

DANAHER, KEVIN (1962), *In Ireland long ago*, Dublin and Cork: Mercier Press.

DANAHER, KEVIN (1966), "King of all Birds", pp 27–30, in *Ireland of the Welcomes*, vol. 15 (4), Nov.–Dec. 1966.

DANAHER, KEVIN (1972), *The Year in Ireland*, Cork: Mercier Press.

DE FUIREASTAIL, MÁIRTÍN (1973), "Hunting the Wran", pp 2–4, in *Treoir*, Vol.5 (6).

DOHMEN, DORIS (1994), *Das deutsche Irlandbild: Imagologische Untersuchungen zur Darstellung Irlands und der Iren in der deutschsprachigen Literatur*, Amsterdam: Rodopi.

DOUGLAS, MARY (1966, ARK ed. 1984), *Purity and Danger: An Analysis of the Concepts of Pollution and Taboo*, London: Routledge & Kegan Paul.

EVANS, ESTYN E. (1957), *Irish Folkways*, London: Routledge & Kegan Paul.

FRASER, TOM (ed.) (2000) *The Irish Parading Tradition*, London: Macmillan.

FRAZER, JAMES G. (1922, PAPERMAC ed. 1987), *The Golden Bough: A Study in Magic and Religion*, London: Macmillan.

GRASS, GÜNTER (1960), *Die Blechtrommel* (The Tin Drum), Frankfurt a.M.: Fischer.

HANNIGAN, STEÁFÁN (1991), *The Bodhrán Book* (pamphlet), Cork: Ossian.

HERZFELD, MICHAEL (1987), *Anthropology Through the Looking-Glass: Critical Ethnography in the Margins of Europe*, Cambridge: Cambridge University Press.

HORNBOSTEL and SACHS (1914), "Systematik der Musikinstrumente: ein Versuch", in *Zeitschrift für Ethnologie*. Translated into English by A. Baines and K.P. Wachsmann as "Classification of Musical Instruments" (1961). Reprinted in *Ethnomusicology: An Introduction* (1992), pp 444–61, ed. H. Myers, London: Macmillan.

HUMPHRIES, JIM (1976), "Making Bodhráns in Ardnaculla", p.19 in *Treoir* 1976 (1).

JARMAN, NEIL (1999), *Displaying Faith: Orange, Green and Trade Union Banners in Northern Ireland*, Belfast: Institute of Irish Studies, Queen's University Belfast.

JARMAN, NEIL (2000), " 'For God and Ulster': Blood and Thunder Bands and Loyalist Political Culture" in Tom Fraser (ed.) *The Irish Parading Tradition*, London: Macmillan.

KATER, MICHAEL H. (1992), *Different Drummers: Jazz in the Culture of Nazi Germany*, New York and Oxford: Oxford University Press.

KEANE, JOHN B. (1986), *The Bodhrán Makers*, Dingle: Brandon Press.

KEARNS, MALACHY BODHRÁN (1996), *Wallup! The Humour and Lore of Bodhrán making*, Connemara: Roundstone Musical Instruments.

KILLEN, JOHN, ed. (1986), *The Second Irish Christmas Book*, Belfast: Blackstaff Press.

LOMAX, ALAN (1968), *Folk Song Style and Culture*, Washington: American Association for the Advancement of Science.

MacCURTAIN, MARGARET and MARY O'DOWD, eds (1991), *Women in Early Modern Ireland*, Dublin: Wolfhound Press.

MacDONALD, SHARON, ed. (1993), *Inside European Identities: Ethnography in Western Europe*, Oxford: Berg.

MAC GRIANNA, SEOSEAMH (1969), *An Druma Mór*, Baile Átha Cliath: Oifig an tSoláthair.

McCRACKEN, CAROL (1996), "A Torrent of Sound", pp 50–2, in *Causeway* (Cultural Traditions Journal), Winter 1996.

McCRICKARD, JANET E. (1987), *The Bodhrán: The Background to the Traditional Irish Drum* (pamphlet), Glastonbury: Fieldfare Arts.

MULLER, SYLVIE (1996-7), "The Irish Wren Tales and Ritual", pp 131–69, in *Béaloideas – The Journal of the Folklore of Ireland Society* vol. 64–65.

Ó DANACHAIR, CAOIMHÍN: see DANAHER, KEVIN

O'DOWD, ANNE and MAIREAD REYNOLDS (1986), "The Wren Hunt", pp 131–5, in *The Second Irish Christmas Book*, ed. John Killen, Belfast: Blackstaff Press.

Ó RIADA, SEÁN (1982), *Our Musical Heritage*, Portlaoise: Fundúireact an Riadaigh/Dolmen Press.

Ó SÚILLEABHÁIN, MÍCHEÁL (1974a/1974b), "The Bodhrán" (part 1 and 2), in *Treoir*, pp 4–7, Vol.6 (2), and pp 6–10, Vol.6 (5).

Ó SÚILLEABHÁIN, MÍCHEÁL (1984), *The Bodhrán: An easy to learn method for the complete beginner, showing the different regional styles and techniques* (pamphlet), Dublin: Walton's.

REILY, SUZEL ANA (1995), "Political Implications of Musical Performance", pp 72–102, in *The World of Music* (Journal of the International Institute for Traditional Music), Vol.37 (2).

REILY, SUZEL ANA (forthcoming), *Voices of the Magi*, Chicago: Chicago University Press.

SCHILLER, RINA (1999), "Gender and traditional Irish music", pp 200–5, in *Crosbhealach an Cheoil –The Crossroads Conference 1996*, eds Fintan Vallely et al.

SCULLION, FIONNUALA (1981), "History and Origins of the Lambeg Drum", pp 19–38, in *Ulster Folklife* (Journal of the UFTM), vol. 27.

SCULLION, FIONNUALA (1982), The Lambeg Drum in Ulster, unpublished MA thesis, Belfast: Queen's University Belfast.

SHAW-SMITH, DAVID (1984), *Ireland's Traditional Crafts*, London: Thames and Hudson.

STOKES, MARTIN ed. (1994), *Ethnicity, Identity and Music: The Musical Construction of Place*, Oxford: Berg.

SUCH, DAVID G. (1985), "The Bodhrán: The Black Sheep in the Family of Traditional Irish Musical Instruments", pp 9–19, in *Galpin Society Journal* vol. 38, April 1985.

VALLELY, FINTAN (1995), "The Drums of War and Peace", *Irish Times*, 12 July 1995.

VALLELY, FINTAN ed. (1999), *The Companion to Irish Traditional Music*, Cork: Cork University Press.

VALLELY, FINTAN and HAMMY HAMILTON, EITHNE VALLELY & LIZ DOHERTY eds (1999), *Crosbhealach an Cheoil –The Crossroads Conference 1996*, Dublin: Whinstone Music/Ossian.

Discography

The Armagh Rhymers (1996), *The Armagh Rhymers,* (own production: educational tape and CD), copies available from: Unit 11, The Old Mill, Kinelowen Street, Keady, Co. Armagh, Northern Ireland, BT60 3SU.

Bradley, Harry (2000), (with Séamus O'Kane), *Bad Turns and Horseshoe Bends*, Outlet Records TTICD 9000.

The Chieftains (1991), *The Bells of Dublin* (The Christmas Album), RCA RD 60824 (CD), RK 60824 (tape).

Clarke, Anthony John (1999), *Man With A Red Guitar*, Terra Nova TERR CD018.

Dennehy, Tim (1993), *A Winter's Tear (Traditional and Original Songs of Love, Loss and Longing)*, Cló Iar-Chonnuachta CIC CD 087.

Dennehy, Tim (1997), *Farewell to Miltown Malbay (Traditional and original songs of love, loss and longing Vol. 2)*, Sceilig Records SRCD 002.

Four Men & A Dog (1991), *Shifting Gravel,* Cross Border Media CBM CD 001.

McConnell, Mickey (2000), *Joined-Up Writing,* Spring Records SCD 1045.

Ó Canainn, Tomás (1985), (with Séamus O'Kane), *New Tunes For Old,* Outlet Records TOC 1 (tape).

O'Rourke, Brian (1992), *When I Grow Up (Jocoserious songs unaccompanied),* Camus Productions (Galway) CP 010 (tape).

Ó Súilleabháin, Mícheál (1992), (with Mel Mercier), *Gaiseadh/Flowing,* Virgin Venture CD VE 915.

Ó Súilleabháin, Mícheál (1995), (with Mel Mercier), *Between Worlds,* Virgin Venture CD VE 926.

Scithereedee (Tim Lyons and Fintan Vallely) (2000), *Big Guns And Hairy Drums*, Whinstone Music WHN 002.

Various (with Séamus O'Kane) (2000), *Crosskeys Inn Life In The Kitchen,* CD (own production), copies available from: Crosskeys Inn, 39 Grange Road, Toomebridge, Co. Antrim, N. Ireland.

Wynne, John (2000), (with Séamus O'Kane), *With Every Breath*, UPROS Music CD 001.

Thanks are due to the musicians whose words and/or music are included here for giving permission for their work to be used in this book.

Index

The page numbers in bold indicate illustrations